A TRINITY HEART NOVEL
BOOK TWO

Trinity Heart
The Guardian

JULIE BRAGONIER MINNICK

Trinity Heart: The Guardian is a work of fiction. Names, characters, places and incidents either are the product of the imagination or are used fictitiously. Any resemblance to actual persons, living or dead, events or locales is entirely coincidental.

Cover art ©2015 by Julie Bragonier Minnick

ISBM-10: 098611121X

ISBM-13: 978-0-9861112-1-1

Dedication

To my dad…who prayed over us every night.

Chapter One

It was late June. School was done for the year and Trinity and Nicholas were sitting aboard the train headed for London. Trinity watched the landscape go by as she pondered Logan's note to her.

"Soon" was all it said. She wondered about it every day. What did it mean? When would she see him? How soon was "soon"? Under what circumstances would she see him again? All these thoughts ran through her head as she heard the click-it-tat rhythm of the train on the track.

"Thinking of him?" her twin brother asked.

"No."

Raised eyebrows.

Smile. More like a smirk.

"Ok, fine...yes," she admitted.

Her brother chuckled.

"He said, 'soon.' Does that mean next week? July, October, next year?" she asked, perplexed.

He shrugged.

"Why couldn't he just give me a date?"

"That wouldn't be any fun."

She gave him a dirty look.

She needed a distraction. She reached inside her backpack, grabbed her iPod and listened to her playlist.

Nicholas plugged his headphones back into his ears. He wondered as well when they would see Logan again. Both of them hoped it was because of something good, not like this past year.

Trinity and her brother stood out among the crowd on the train. They had raven black hair. Hers long and unruly, his wavy and appealing. They shared crystal blue eyes that stood out against pallid skin. Trinity always had apple red lips, while Nicholas had naturally pink lips. The two of them were striking, especially when they were together.

She looked down at her black and white plaid skirt, with a few chains hanging off the side. She had her thigh-high socks slouched down a bit since it was warm, and her combat boots laced three-quarters the way up. Her brother dressed more "European gothic" with military overtones.

As the English countryside zoomed past Trinity began to let her mind wander. She wondered when she should make the trip to

Oxford University to see if she liked the campus. Even though Trinity and Nicholas were Americans, she really liked the U.K. and planned on finishing her education here.

Trinity started to doze off. As she did, she sensed something was wrong. She jerked upright and looked around. No one else sensed it. She felt a rhythm that was amiss. She paused. The click-it-tat had changed. She ripped her headphones off. Sure enough, something was wrong. She grabbed her brother's arm. Immediately he tore off his headphones. He knew his sister well enough to know something was very wrong.

"What?" he asked, anxiously.

"The train," was all she said before there was a loud screeching sound.

The twins grasped each other and braced themselves.

Trinity quickly threw out a whispered "protect us!"

The train started to bend to-and-fro. It wobbled on the track. The twins knew it was going to crash. They held hands, ducked down in their seats and braced themselves. Trinity kept calling out for protection in a desperate small voice.

Logan once told her it was her super-power, the ability to make angels come to her beck and call. Having seen it work and save her life once before, she now believed it.

The trains whistle howled. Children screamed. Women cried. Trinity whispered amidst the terror and horror. She just kept praying.

"Protect us. Protect Us. Protect Us."

She had faith that they would walk away from this crash. She did not know why, but she had seen enough in the past year to know she could survive anything. She had a purpose on earth and it did not include dying today.

The last car on the train jumped the track. The twins could see the last car swinging back and forth being dragged behind the train. Then the second to the last car jumped the track. People screamed. The train was now dragging two cars. The car the twins were in was next. Screeching of metal on metal, grinding of brakes, wailing of people. Catastrophe was inevitable.

BAM! The twins' car took flight and the three loose cabins flipped sideways. Trinity and her brother were thrown across the car. The windows shattered, luggage and belongings flew out some of the windows. The twins crawled to their seats which were flipped sideways and tried to hold on. Trinity had an idea and she and her brother curled up in the luggage rack.

One word escaped her lips over and over, "protect." Even through the chaos she was faithful to chant her request. They bumped up and down as the car on its side was dragged down the track. Trinity wondered how long it would be before the entire train dumped over.

The brakes were grinding, the screech of metal grew louder. It felt like an eternity before the train slowed down. Just when Trinity thought they were going to make it, the entire train tore from the track and rolled-over once as it tumbled down the embankment. The twins were tossed about as the car slid. Finally the train came to a halt.

5

There was silence, but only for one moment. Then people inside the cars started yelling.

"Get out of the train!"

Trinity looked around to make sure everyone was capable of getting out of the train. It looked as if no one was injured where they could not move. Trinity and Nicholas climbed over the seats and out one of the windows. They jumped off the train and rolled down the grassy hill. They looked back to see people pouring out of the trains. Everyone was running to get their distance because they saw smoke coming from the engine car.

Men ran from group to group and asked if everyone was out of the train. Each car was cleared and the passengers were a safe distance away when they all stared at the wreckage. The twisted train lay piled in a heap. Nicholas wrapped his arms around his twin sister. She sighed a breath of relief.

KABOOM! The engine car exploded. They leapt back, startled as the heap of iron blazed. Burning diesel fumes and angry smoke rose to the sky. Trinity gasped. In the distance she heard sirens. Fire trucks, ambulances, police were all on the way to help.

Nicholas looked around and then at his sister. The twins thought the same thing at the same time.

"Mom's going to freak out!"

They chuckled. They were twins, they had that connection where they could sense each other, think the same things, say the same things, and finish each other's sentences.

The police arrived and began to make sure everyone got off the train alive and that everyone was accounted for. Medics attended to injuries. Trinity and Nicholas had some scrapes and bruises but nothing was broken. There were others than needed immediate medical attention more than they did.

Eventually, Trinity and her brother were put on a bus heading to London. Their very worried parents would pick them up at the station. Trinity looked out the window.

What a way to start the summer.

Chapter Two

"Trinity! Nicholas!" They heard their names called out as they got off the bus. They turned to see their parents across the station. The four ran to each other's arms. Their mom and dad embraced them and squeezed tightly.

They knew their parents were worried sick when they heard of the wreck. They all loaded into the car and headed for their townhouse in London. The twins lost their suitcases in the crash. They were just glad to be alive and unharmed.

Trinity's mom could not let go of her hand. She kept squeezing it and looking back relieved to see her twins in the back seat. Once they reached their townhouse, everyone plopped down in the family room and the twins filled in their parents on everything that happened at the train crash.

Their parents were extremely glad they were okay. Over dinner, take-away Indian food, they talked about the school year. The twins told their parents about their new friends, Logan, Alaina, Phoenix and Tristan. Trinity's dad teased her about Logan. He knew she and Logan had "kind-of" dated through the school year. Trinity told her parents she really hoped he would be in London this summer so they could meet him.

The twins conveniently left out the parts about the demons, angels, the fighting, and the blood. They had agreed to leave out everything that was not explainable, or Roan's attack on Trinity and her miraculous healing. She had rehearsed how she was going to explain her fresh tattoos. She decided it was better to just get it over with.

"So…this past year I've been studying the different aspects of angels," she started to explain to her parents. They nodded, listening.

"I've really been intrigued by the idea, the possibilities and it's really started to become important to me," she continued.

"It's become a…" Trinity searched for the right word.

"Quest for knowledge?" her mother suggested.

Trinity grinned and nodded.

"Exactly, a quest to figure out what I think, what information there is about them, even finding myself in all of it," she said.

Nicholas chimed in.

"Trinity has been soul-searching."

9

"Sounds like an interesting topic to be curious about, Trinity," her dad said.

So far, so good. She was thrilled her parents were approving. Now came the hard part.

"So in all of this, I've had real moments of clarity and wanted to mark those moments in my life."

Her mom grinned, "You got a tattoo."

It was a statement, not a question.

Trinity nodded and grimaced, expecting a little bit of tongue-lashing.

"Well I would have liked you to wait until you were eighteen, but I guess you're close enough."

Trinity sighed with relief. She knew her parents were not going to be too upset. They had tattoos and always encouraged self-expression. She showed her parents the angel wings at the nape of her neck. And then she showed them the black, velvety feather across one side of her upper ribs.

What her parents did not know was that the black feather was where the demon, Roan, had torn into her side with his sharp teeth. When Logan and his angelic friends healed her, the next morning the tattooed feather had been there in the place of a scar. It was a reminder of the miracle that had occurred in her life.

The angel wings on the back of her neck and been a Christmas gift to Logan to remember him by. She never wanted to forget this year of her life. It had changed who she was and who she was going to be.

Her mom gave her a hug.

"You know that you should have asked permission first, but I understand why you did it," she said as she kissed her forehead.

"Remember, the journey is more important than the milestones."

Trinity hugged her mom back. Her mom obviously did not know the whole story.

"I know mom," said Trinity, "But some milestones are worth remembering."

The twins went to get ready for bed. It had been a long day and they needed to sleep it off.

Trinity lay in bed looking at the ceiling. She knew that when she offered up her whispered prayers that Logan could hear her. It was like her own homemade soup-can-with-a-sting telephone.

"Thank you for the protection. Let me see Logan soon. Goodnight."

Chapter Three

The twins slept in. It was summer vacation and they had no need to wake up early. Trinity rolled out of bed in her black and white striped pajama pants and black tank top. Her dad was cooking pancakes from scratch on the griddle, along with sausage and bacon. They might live in the U.K., but they were going to eat like Americans.

"Morning sleepy-head," he said, warmly.

She grinned. She forgot how much she missed her dad when she was away at school.

"You sore at all? Anything hurt from the crash yesterday?" he asked.

"So-so," she answered.

"What's so-so?" her brother asked, yawning and stretching as he crawled onto the barstool.

"You better not be talking about my cooking," her dad joked.

They all chuckled.

Trinity closed her eyes and sucked in the yummy aroma of bacon and pancakes. It smelled like home and everything was good now that they were all together for the summer.

Trinity and Nicholas attended Shadowland Academy, a boarding school in the country-side of England. Both their parents were American spies employed by the CIA. They were not supposed to know this piece of information, but they had found out a few years ago and learned to accept that their parents had a duty to their country. It was exciting at the same time, but hard that they only saw their parents every few months.

Trinity shook her unruly, raven hair. Even in her pajamas, and without her beloved eyeliner, she was striking. Their mom walked in, gave her kids a big bear hug and they all sat down for a late, very late, breakfast. The family talked as if they had never been away from each other.

Trinity and Nicholas needed to buy some clothes for the summer since their luggage was destroyed. They all decided to head out for the afternoon and spend some time together.

While out shopping, Trinity and Nicholas bought clothes here and there. Trinity kept her closet simple with black, white, gray and red. She really did not vary from that color palette. She found some plaid, pleated skirts at a small alternative shop, along with some black and gray shorts. She still had her combat boots but she bought a few other pairs of shoes.

They found a street market and browsed through books, records and oddities. They bought food from sidewalk vendors and ate as they shopped. Trinity found an antique book about spiritual beings and bought it. As she was browsing through some unique feathers and jewelry, her brother pointed at a poster plastered on the side of the brick building.

"Check that out," he said, taking a bite of his ice cream.

She looked to where he was pointing. There was a poster for a music competition.

"That would be fun to go to," she said.

"Go to?" he asked, sarcastically.

"Ya, check out the local musicians and see what's new and fresh."

"I'm not going to go check out other musicians. You need to enter."

She laughed.

"Whatever."

"Not 'whatever'. You're good."

"Not good enough for a public competition."

"You won't know if you don't try," Nicholas said.

"Whatever," she repeated, and playfully smacked him.

They trotted off to catch up with their parents. After a few more minutes of browsing, Nicholas brought up the music competition again.

"You really should think about it," Nicholas said.

"I'm not ready for something at that level."

"Trinity, you are good. You are really, really good."

14

She smiled.

"How good?" she asked. "Evanescence good?"

"Trinity good."

"Ha ha," she said, wryly.

"Seriously."

"Seriously," she said, mocking.

He sighed.

"Just think about it."

"Ya ya."

Silence.

"So?" he asked.

"So what?" she asked.

"So, you thought about it yet?"

She chuckled. He threw his arm around her shoulders. And together they walked down the colorful and lively streets of London.

Chapter Four

Later that week, Trinity was curled up in a big arm chair reading the book she had bought at the street market. Her father came in and sat down with the newspaper. She noticed the headline read, "Mysterious beams of light at Stonehenge". She could not take her eyes off the photo of Stonehenge on the front. She had been there before. The mysteries that surrounded its origins intrigued her, what sparked her interest was the "beams of light".

She had seen those lights before. Earlier that year when Logan and his three friends were in the woods and started chanting, a silvery beam of light glowed from earth heavenward. It sparkled in the night as a diamond sparkles in the sunlight. She wondered if this light beam that was seen at Stonehenge was something similar.

Nicholas came into the room and tossed his sister a square envelope. She put her book down and looked at the envelope. She recognized the hand-writing. This past spring, after Logan had left, she had received a note like this. She tore it open and looked at the blank front. Inside, it read, "Soon." There was a black feather embossed below it.

She gasped. Her father looked up.

"Something wrong?"

"Not something wrong, something good," she exclaimed.

Her dad looked at her expectantly. Nicholas gave her a look that said, "Don't say the wrong thing."

"My friend Logan is coming soon. I think he might be visiting London this summer."

Nicholas let out a silent sigh of relief.

She gave him a smug look. A look that said, "I am not an amateur."

He stuck his tongue out at her.

Trinity's dad glanced up from his newspaper and smiled.

"You'll have to bring this young man around so we can meet him."

She nodded and ran out of the room to ponder the newest letter. She ran her finger over the embossed black feather. It had been several months since she received the first note. She wondered if "soon" really meant "soon." Logan was, after all, thousands of years old. So his version of "soon" could be different than hers.

Nicholas came into her bedroom and sat down, tossing his feet up, arms behind his head.

"So?" he asked smugly.

"So," she said, matter-of-fact.

"What it say?"

"What did what say?" she teased.

"The note."

"What note?"

He smirked at her.

"Soon."

"Soon?"

"Soon."

"So how soon, is soon?" he asked.

She shrugged.

"Hopefully sooner than the last soon."

He chuckled.

Silence. She pondered the possibilities.

"We need a diversion," he said.

"From what?"

"From how long we have to wait until soon."

"What do you propose?"

"The music competition!" he said, as if he had just thought of it.

She sighed and rolled her eyes.

"Well?" he asked.

"Ya ya, maybe."

"Really?" he asked, excited.

"I think I'd like to try."

Nicholas jumped up and hugged his sister.

"You are going to be amazing."

Trinity grabbed her brother and dragged him down the stairs and out the front door.

"Where are we going?" he asked, as she dragged him down Shaftesbury.

"To find out where we sign up," she answered.

He stopped.

"Yesterday was the deadline to sign up," he said.

She stopped and looked at him.

"How do you know?"

"The poster said."

"If you knew that, then why did you tell me to sign up today?"

"Cuz," he said, sheepishly.

"N...I...C...H...O...L...A...S?" she said, in a drawn out voice.

"W...H...A...T?" he answered, mimicking her.

"What is going on?"

Silence.

He had a silly grin on his face.

"You didn't?" she asked, realizing exactly what was going on.

His silly grin turned sheepish.

"I kinda did."

"When?"

"Several days ago."

She gave him a playful smack.

19

Nicholas had signed Trinity up for the competition without her knowing about it. He figured he could get her to come around and say "yes" at some point.

"When is the competition?" she asked.

"Friday night. Our friends are in town and are going to come over to practice so you can figure out what you want to sing," Nicholas told her.

"You just thought of everything didn't you," she said, smartly.

"Yup."

"Hmmm," she said.

"Yup."

Chapter Five

The evening was festive and the park was lined with booths. Crowds milled around waiting for the music competition to start. The stage was set up and ready. Trinity wore a black tulle dress with a sash around her waist. She had found it at a vintage store in Soho. She wore her combat boots and her raven black hair hung wavy down her back.

Her brother squeezed her hand.

"Relax," he whispered.

She smiled at him.

"I'm fine."

"Is that why you are shaking?"

"I'm fine."

"And your hands are cold," he added.

"I'm fine."

"And clammy?"

Trinity rolled her eyes.

"Fine. I'm a little nervous."

Kids ran by with long streams of ribbon on sticks swirling in the air. Clowns on stilts walked around entertaining people. Soon everyone began to move towards the stage.

"Well, it's your big night. Go get 'em sis!" he cheered her on.

Trinity took a deep breath and headed back stage. She was scheduled to play last. She sat in the back with her band, waiting. She watched the acts before her play. They were all good. Each a different style, but nothing similar to her haunting, alternative rock. She had picked a song that she wrote after Logan left. It started out quiet and then broke into hard-core Within Temptation style rock.

From back stage she could see her brother close to the front. What had he gotten her into? She was on stage next and she thought she was going to puke.

She whispered a little prayer.

"Give me peace."

She took a deep breath, closed her eyes and focused. She felt a calm come over her. She was confident and ready. She could do this. She had performed before. This was no different than standing in front of her school at the Christmas talent performance.

Suddenly they were calling her name. She walked onto the stage. It was dimly lit. She started humbly and haunting. Her accompaniment started, she closed her eyes and began to sing. A clear angelic voice came out. The crowd hushed and everyone listened attentively. She captured the audience's attention. Who was this pretty girl that sang like a seraph? The song broke out, her band rocked, the stage lights came up and Trinity opened her eyes. The moment was magical.

She smiled at her brother who was standing in the front row. He stuck his tongue out at her as if to say, "I told you so." She loved it. She looked over the crowd but could not see much. But she saw a sea of faces staring back at her. The sky was dark, the stars were out. The carnival buzzed around her and Trinity was the star of the show.

Her song came to a close and the crowd erupted. It was clear she was going to win the competition. She grinned and took a bow. She looked down at her brother who gave her a thumbs up.

The announcer came on the stage and announced that by a clear margin, Trinity had won the competition. Her brother was in the wings waiting to give her a hug. He had to push her back onto the stage to accept the award and to greet her new screaming fans. Winning this meant she went on to the next level of the competition. She smiled shyly. It felt good to win.

As the lights passed over the crowd, she gasped. She thought she saw Logan, but instantly he was gone. Her hopes let down.

Trinity ran to the sidelines and gave her brother another hug. He grabbed her hand.

"Come on, we've got to tell mom and dad."

As Nicholas dragged her through the crowd she caught a glimpse of Logan's look-alike again. She strained to see him as someone walked between them and he was gone. She pulled from her brother's grip and moved toward where she had seen Logan. Her brother called after her as the crowd separated them.

Logan was not there. She looked around in search of his beautiful face. Kids running by with cotton candy, teens sheepishly holding hands, sparklers, clowns, but no Logan. All the merriment of the carnival was missed by Trinity as she searched for her angel.

Nicholas finally caught up with her.

"What?"

"Logan," she said.

"Where?"

She shook her head, puzzled.

"Where'd you see him?"

"Here," came Logan's voice from behind her.

Trinity spun around and grinned shyly.

Logan put his arms around her and she squeezed him tightly. The world disappeared and it was just the two of them. She felt warm, peaceful and giggly.

"Soon, really meant 'soon' this time," she teased.

"I never really know how soon I'll be dispatched, but I wanted to give you hope," he told her.

Nicholas gave Logan a brotherly hug.

"How long are you here in London for?" she asked.

"Don't know."

"What are you here for?"

"Can't tell you that," he said.

"You mean I have to figure it out."

He chuckled.

"I mean I can't tell you...yet"

Nicholas ran off to find their parents leaving the two love-birds alone.

They strolled through the carnival. A fire breather almost singed them. Logan pulled her out of the way as the two of them laughed. They walked down the brightly lit, colorful streets.

Trinity looked over at Logan, swooning on the inside. He had curly light brown hair and blue eyes. He was ruggedly handsome and was built like a warrior. "Of course he was built like a warrior," she thought. He was a warrior angel after all. He fought battles and waged war against the demons. He was her very own superhero. He was so beautiful, he almost glowed. She was giddy with excitement.

Trinity glanced over at him and suddenly jolted. She saw a vision, a waking dream. Logan was dressed as a warrior. His body was war torn from battle, bloody and yet victorious. Then the vision lapsed and she saw him as he was. She tried to shake it off. She did not know what the vision meant. She never had one like that before.

"Where have you been?" she asked, but certain he would not tell her.

He looked at her with a wry grin.

"I know, I know, you can't tell me," she said.

"Sorry," he whispered.

"So, you can't tell me where you've been, you can't tell me what you're doing here or how long you'll be here," she said, playfully. "What can you tell me?"

25

"That I'm here now," he offered, sheepishly. "And I missed you."

She smiled at him.

He took her hand and they walked through the carnival. Tonight was a good night.

Chapter Six

The next morning Trinity bolted straight up out of bed. She remembered the last night's events. She had won the music competition and Logan had come back. Last night he walked her home and promised they would meet up today. She threw back her covers, got dressed in her usual black, white and red and ran down the stairs. Her dad was in his usual chair reading the paper.

"In a hurry are we?" he asked, amused.

"Logan is in London and we are going over to see him and our friends today," she said, excited.

"That sounds like fun. Do I get to meet this Mr. Logan?" her dad asked, tending to his paper.

Trinity went over and plopped into her dad's lap.

27

"Yes. He is coming by to pick Nicholas and me up in a few minutes."

Her dad gave her a big hug.

"I'm sure I will love him."

"I'm sure you will," she replied.

"You did amazing job last night Trinity. We are very proud of you."

"I kind of surprised myself," she admitted.

"When is the next part of the competition?" he asked.

"I don't know. I wasn't really paying attention. Got kind of distracted," she said, with a funny grin.

"You think?" her dad jested.

"Yup."

"Hmmm."

Knock. Knock. Knock.

Trinity jumped up.

"He's here!"

She ran to the front door and opened it.

"Hey," she said, almost shyly.

Pause.

"Come in and meet my parents," she said.

Logan entered the townhouse. Trinity's dad stood up and put his paper aside.

"You must be Logan."

"Mr. Heart," he said, respectfully.

"Trinity has told us a lot about you."

"Do you mind if she and Nicholas spend the day with me, my brother and a couple friends from school?" Logan asked. "My townhouse is in Covent Garden."

"Sounds good to me," her dad said. "Why don't you guys all come back here for dinner so we can get to know you, your brother and friends?"

"Yes sir."

"Have fun," her dad said as he sat down in his chair and picked up the paper.

"Nicholas!" Trinity yelled up the stairs.

He came down and gave Logan a fist pump.

"Later dad," Nicholas called out as they ran out the front door.

"Is everybody really here?" Trinity asked.

"All four of us."

Logan, Nicholas and Trinity walked through the side streets and through Covent Garden to Logan's apartment. When he opened the door Alaina flew at Trinity and gave her a big hug.

"Oh my gosh, I've missed you," Alaina said.

She had maroon-red, thick hair. Her green eyes sparkled as she grabbed Nicholas and gave him a hug as well. Trinity saw Tristan, Logan's older brother and walked up and gave him a quick casual hug. Tristan looked like his brother, except his hair was darker.

Phoenix also gave Trinity a hug and Nicholas a fist pump. He had brown hair and his green eyes stood out against his brown skin.

29

The twins and these four angels had shared a lot in the past year. Trinity and Nicholas had helped them defeat Zoenn, Roan and the other demons. During that time Logan and Trinity had a shared crush that neither of them could explain. They knew pursuing it was complicated.

Trinity found Logan beautiful and strong. He was unlike any other guy she had ever met, but then again…he was not just a guy; he was her "snow angel" as she had labeled him last year when they first met. Logan thought Trinity was unique and striking. She was independent, confident and had a vivacious will to do something great with her life.

The two of them stared at one another. Trinity was almost jumping out of her skin. She could not believe she was here with Logan, finally.

"So what's up?" Nicholas asked.

"You guys are here for more than just summer break," Trinity said.

Silence.

"Come on; tell us what is going on?" Trinity begged.

The angels looked at each other and grinned.

"Seriously, you didn't bring us here to just shop."

"How bad is it?" Nicholas asked.

Trinity got serious real fast.

"Is Roan back?" she asked, inquiring about a demon that had been at their school last year in human form. He had taken a liking to Trinity and haunted her all year.

"Yes we are here for a reason," Logan began.

"It's not good," Alaina added, seriously.

"There is a disturbance at Stonehenge," Logan added. Stonehenge is a rock monument in a small town outside of London. Its origin is unknown to the human race.

"We are here to prepare for whatever is going to happen."

"What does Stonehenge have to do with it?" Trinity asked, wondering if she was going to be one of the first humans in this time period to learn what Stonehenge was all about.

The angels all looked at one another.

"This is completely confidential and you are never to repeat it. Stonehenge has been a secret since ancient times," Tristan warned.

"Not all demons can take human form like Roan and the others did last year. Usually they have to take possession of a human and not materialize as humans themselves," said Logan.

Trinity kind-of understood. She had studied this in the large ancient book she had found last year. The book is where she had seen the drawings of Warrior angels' tattoo markings. That was how she figured out that Logan and the others were angels. She had seen his tattoos at a swim practice and then confronted him about it.

Logan continued, "Stonehenge is a portal for our realm. Demons can use the portal to enter the human realm. Once, a long time ago, Stonehenge portal was open and many demons entered the human realm and took human hosts. There was a huge battle, the angels won and closed the portal. Ever since then, angels have been guarding the portal; they watch over it and make sure that it stays closed."

Trinity stared at Logan. She was overwhelmed and excited all at the same time. The idea that Stonehenge was a portal excited her. But the fact that Logan and the others were here because something was going wrong and they needed to help keeping the portal safe worried her.

"So what is going on with the portal?" she asked.

"We don't know exactly. We know something is coming, but we don't know what and when," Alaina offered.

"What are you guys supposed to do?" Nicholas asked.

"Watch, wait and gather information," was the answer.

"Are you telling me 1,000 Roans could fly through the portal?" Trinity asked, horrified at the idea of demons entering the human realm.

"We aren't going to let that happen," Logan assured her.

"So what can we do to help?" she asked.

"When we know, we will tell you," Tristan offered.

Chapter Seven

The whole gang entered Trinity and Nicholas' kitchen. Introductions were made. Their parents only knew these were friends of their kids from school. The "angel" part was kept a secret.

Trinity's mom smiled knowingly at Logan and Trinity as they openly stared at one another, much too often. She seated everyone around the kitchen table and served up spaghetti, meatballs, Italian salad and garlic bread. Trinity's dad said grace, which she thought was pretty ironic.

Dinner went smoothly. Everyone laughed and had a good time.

"Trinity mentioned you guys moved here from New Zealand, how long were you there?" Trinity's mom asked.

"About a year," Logan offered.

"Your parents' military or you guys just move around a lot?" she asked.

"Military," Tristan said.

Trinity's dad asked a lot of questions and got to know Logan and the others. He liked what he saw. By the end of dinner Mr. Heart knew that his kids had found some great friends. Even though he had just met them, he had a great feeling about them.

After Trinity and Nicholas had said goodnight to their guests and headed to bed, Trinity's mom looked at Mr. Heart.

"Good kids," she said, assured.

"Ya. The twins found some great friends," he replied.

"Think Logan will stick around? Trinity is quite taken with him."

"For her sake, I hope so," he answered.

"Sounds like at least he will be around for the summer."

"Ah….summer love," Mr. Heart teased.

Mrs. Heart smacked him with the dish towel and giggled.

The next morning Trinity was up and ready bright and early. Logan was coming to take her to a street market so they could spend time together. Without fail, he was on time. She darted out the door.

He took her hand in his. She looked up shyly at him. It was like the relationship was new all over again. The tingles, the romance, the butterflies, it was exciting.

34

"He chose me," she kept telling herself.

As if he could read her thoughts he stopped in the middle of the street, pulled her to him and caressed her chin with the back of his fingers, then held it in his palm.

"What have you done to me, Ms. Heart?"

As if on cue, a street band up on the stage starting singing a rendition of "I put a spell on you."

"Hmmm. Guess that answers my question."

He placed a gentle kiss on her lips. She grinned. He chuckled.

"We'll have to try that later," he smirked.

They strolled through the market hand in hand looking at trinkets and food made by locals. One of the booths they stopped at had antique jewelry. Trinity was memorized by an Egyptian ring. The gypsy woman explained it was over 300 years old and found in Cairo. It sparkled. Logan grinned and bought it.

"But it was so expensive," she complained.

"Really? I don't have a concept for money since it's not something we really need or use," Logan explained.

Logan smirked.

"I guess not."

Logan placed the ring on her finger and crooned, "She wears an Egyptian ring that sparkles before she speaks."

"Who sings that?"

"Bob Dylan."

"I might have to re-write that song in my style," Logan mused.

"You're going to re-write a Bob Dylan song? Sacrilege!"

She giggled.

"That bad huh?"

He kissed her forehead.

"If anyone could do it, you could."

They spent the morning continuing to browse. Lunch was spent at a little pub that had a restaurant seating area outside. They watched the world go by.

"So you don't know how long I get to keep ya and you have work to do," she whined.

He looked at her with a serious expression.

"You are a part of this."

"What? How?" she wanted to know.

"Everything will be revealed in time. Even I don't know all the details yet," he explained. "I just want you to be ready to understand and accept when it all comes to fruition."

She looked at him wondering if this was why he chose her. She looked at her hands. He picked up on her mood.

"How could I possibly know you were connected to all this last year when we came to school to help with the Dark Ones? I didn't even know you existed before I came to England."

What he said made sense and she trusted his assurances.

He grinned wryly.

"I don't know how I didn't know about you, because you are the most amazing girl I've ever met." Cheeky grin. "And I've met my fair share of girls…considering I've been around since the beginning of time."

She swatted at him.

"I don't want to hear about your previous girlfriends."

"What previous girlfriends?" he asked. "I've never fallen for a human before."

"Never?" she asked.

"Never."

"Wait, you just said you've never fallen for a human before. Have you fallen for an angel before?"

He grinned.

She playfully smacked him again.

"Well I don't want to hear about that either," she said, with a chuckle.

"I will keep it to myself."

She squinted at him suspiciously.

"Why in the world would I want to hear about your eternally beautiful, previous girlfriend, when we both know that someday my beauty will fade as I age," she said, smartly.

"Touché," he said. "Touché."

Smack.

Chapter Eight

The next day the twins and angels went out. Trinity wanted to visit the art museum in London where she saw the painting of her four angel friends. They were not too thrilled to see themselves immortalized again. But they agreed that Trinity would go look at the painting while they all hung around at other paintings just in case someone recognized them and started asking questions.

Last year Trinity was at the museum on a field trip with Logan and one of the paintings in the museum had Tristan, Alaina, Logan and Phoenix in it, painted as angels. Apparently a few hundred years ago someone else saw the foursome and decided to paint what he had seen.

As they walked through the museum once in a while the four angels would chuckle.

"What's so funny?" Nicholas asked.

"That painting is titled, 'Arch Angel Michael' and he doesn't look anything like," Tristan said.

"In fact, if he saw that, I think he would be quite offended," Alaina said, chuckling.

"Why?"

"That's a pretty ugly looking angel," she offered. "Michael is stunning! Most humans that have seen him ogle and drool over him."

"So you're saying that artist didn't actually see Michael," Trinity joked.

"Uh, heck no."

They arrived at the painting that featured the twin's angelic friends. The two of them went over and studied the painting. Sure enough, there was the foursome, in all their beauty, in a scene assisting a human. It always amazed Trinity and reminded her that Logan really was a couple thousand years old. It almost put a damper on her mood, once again bringing up the ever somber question, "where can this relationship go?"

When she was done, they all headed over to the park where old movies played on a large sheet. They bought their goodies and settled down to watch," Singing in the rain."

Logan spent the evening with his arm safely around Trinity. She snuggled in the crook of his shoulder. She never wanted the moment to end.

Once the movie was over, Logan walked Trinity home, privately. He stopped in the ally of London's China Town.

Lanterns were lit, the stores shown their well-lit Chinese symbols advertising fresh duck. He pulled her aside. She thought he was going to kiss her.

"I have to go for a while," he blurted out.

"So soon?" she asked, fearful.

"I'll be back. But we have to go report to Michael and get further orders," he explained. "Problem is, I feel this need to protect you. But I'm not a protector angel, I'm a warrior."

"I know," she said, kinda girly. She liked that he was a warrior angel. It made him feel safe and manly.

"If I can, I'll send someone to watch over you," he offered. "And you know how to bring angels to your beck and call," he reminded her.

She knew that all she needed to do was pray and angels would be dispatched to her need. She had realized that last year when she started having dreams of Roan attacking her. Once she realized she just needed to call out in prayer for Logan to come to her side, he was there. Same thing on the train, even though she could not see them, she knew angels were there keeping her safe when it jumped the track.

Logan walked her to her door.

"I will be back."

"How Arnold Schwarzenegger of you," she giggled.

He just rolled his eyes.

Kiss.

He was gone.

Chapter Nine

A week went by and Trinity was bored. The four angels were gone and Nicholas and Trinity were left to wonder what was going on.

Trinity spent hours in her room writing new songs. She was preparing for the next phase of the competition she had won a few weeks earlier. Her latest song was dark and haunting. She wrote from feeling the loss of Logan. Even though she knew he was coming back she tried to optimize the darker feelings into music.

Every day she felt as though she was being watched. She sensed another presence. It was a comforting presence, like someone watching over her. She began to wonder if Logan had sent a Protector to watch over her.

One night she was walking back from the music store where she had her guitar restrung and she had that feeling again. She stopped. The ally was lined with brick buildings. The street lights glowed and lit the road. No one was around.

She put her guitar down and leaned against the brick wall. She could hear people milling about Covent Garden. London was lively till the wee hours of the morning. There were locals and tourists pouring out of theaters and restaurants. She waited.

Silence.

She felt a presence next to her; almost as if it was leaning against the wall with her. She steadied her breathing and tuned into what she felt. It did not feel evil. It was not a danger to her. But she was not sure what it was.

Silence.

Finally she spoke up.

"I know you are there. Why not just show yourself? It will make this a whole lot easier."

She waited.

Nothing.

It was bizarre but she could sense hesitation in whatever it was that accompanied her.

Sigh.

"Come on. I don't bite," she joked.

Nothing.

She felt the presence move. It no longer was beside her but in front of her, almost face to face.

"Please," she whispered, assuring. "If Logan sent you, then you know that I know of your existence."

Silence.

"So why not just show yourself? I know you are there. I am going to talk to you and I will look a whole lot saner if I am not talking to an imaginary friend."

She waited.

She felt the presence move away from her.

"Don't go," she whispered.

Trinity slowly picked up her guitar and turned to walk out of the ally, but stopped when she sensed the presence behind her. She felt warm breath on her neck.

She did not look over her shoulder.

"You there?" she whispered, breathless with anticipation.

"Yes," came a tentative, but friendly voice.

"May I turn around?"

"Ya," he said, shyly.

She put the guitar down and slowly turned. She was face to face with a boy near her own age. He was a few inches taller than her. His hair was curly and golden blonde. His eyes ocean blue.

"How'd you know?" he asked, in wonder.

"I felt you."

Silence.

"Who are you?" she asked.

"Samuel."

"I mean, what are you?"

He smiled.

43

She looked at him suspiciously with a wry grin.

"Your protector," he smirked.

She rolled her eyes.

"No I'm serious," he said, smiling. "Logan sent me to watch out for you."

She became suspicious.

"So you thought sneaking around unseen was the best approach?" she asked, playfully.

"Well, that's kinda what we do, ya know."

"Ya I guess marching up to someone and announcing, 'Hey I'm your protector angel, may I tag along?' wouldn't go so well."

He shrugged in response.

"You know I've seen Logan right?" she asked him.

He nodded.

"So what's the harm in revealing yourself to me?" she said, with a grin.

Samuel gave her a mischievous grin.

"Logan told me not to," he said.

"Why?" she asked, confused.

"Guess he wants to keep you for himself." Samuel teased.

She swatted him playfully.

"Sammy huh?"

"Samuel."

"Sam?"

"I can live with that."

"So what now?" she asked.

"Well, I can keep shadowing you unseen or...."

44

"I'll take the or," she responded.

"Guess we're palling around together till Logan gets back then."

"Well Pal Sammy…"

"Sam."

"Right, Pal Sam, I'm going to go home, get into my pajamas and get some sleep and it would go over better with my parents if you weren't there watching me."

He laughed.

"You realize I'll just go unseen to watch over you in your sleep," he teased.

"Eek!" she said. "Is there an 'OR' for this as well?"

He shrugged.

"I come home as one of your brother's friends and stay with Nicholas till Logan comes back."

"So you can be near, but not hovering," she said.

"Exactly!" His eyes gleamed with delight.

"Man I hope Nicholas takes the cues when I walk in with you."

The two walked back to the Heart's townhouse. Standing outside the front door Trinity looked Sam over.

"Uh…you got any luggage? Not sure I can sell this 'friend coming to visit' story without it."

He grinned.

"I'll have it."

She raised an eyebrow.

"Okey doke Pal Sam….whatever you say."

They walked into the house.

"Nicholas!" Trinity yelled out.

Her twin ran down the stairs as her parents came out of the kitchen.

"You forget to pick someone up at the train station?" she asked, trying to get her brother to catch on.
Nicholas looked at her quizzically while her parents looked on. Samuel walked through the front door with a duffle bag.

"I ran into Sam down by the bus stop on my way home, he was looking for our house since you forgot to pick him up at the train station."

Nicholas caught on.

"Sam! Oh my word, I totally forgot. So sorry bro." He gave his 'so-called friend' a big hug and took his duffle.

"Mom, dad, I totally forgot I invited a friend from school to come stay with me for…a while." Nicholas said to his parents.

Samuel reached out and shook Mr. and Mrs. Heart's hands.

"Pleasure to meet you."

"It's our pleasure to have you here," Mrs. Heart said, warmly.

"Come on Sam, let's get you settled in."

Trinity, Samuel and Nicholas ran up the stairs. Once in Nicholas' room, he just stood staring at his sister waiting for an explanation.

"Nicholas. Sam. Sam. Nicholas." Introductions made.

"And…." Her twin asked.

"Logan sent me a Protector."

"The ethereal kind I'm assuming." Nicholas chuckled.

Sam nodded.

"He's yours at night and mine during the day."

"Ya having him stay in your room would be a hard sell to mom and dad," Nicholas joked.

"And I don't want him hovering over me in invisible land."

"Ok. Night night Sammy."

"Night."

She left.

The boys grinned at each other.

Chapter Ten

In the morning Trinity found a red rose next to her bed. She was not sure who left it there or where it came from. There was a little note that said, "Good Morning!"

She went into the boy's room with the rose in hand.

"Did either of you leave this by my bed?" she asked. They both shrugged.

"You found that next to your bed?" her brother asked.

"Yes."

"Was your window open?" Sam asked.

"Nope."

Both boys looked perplexed.

"Apparently you have a secret admirer," Nicholas teased.

"I got that much. The question is, how did he get it into my room?"

Both boys shrugged again.

Trinity shrugged as well.

"Oh well, let's go to Stonehenge," she said, prancing out of the room to get ready.

Samuel was not so keen on the idea but there was not much he could do to stop them. The three of them bought train tickets to Salisbury, and then they would take a bus out to Stonehenge. The twins had been there before. It had always interested them, but now it intrigued them even more because they knew its true purpose.

"I've been here twice and never really felt any spiritual presence before," Trinity said while they sat on the bus.

"Depends on when you come out here," Sam explained.

"How so?" she asked.

"Well, there are dormant stages with not much spiritual activity. And then there are times with lots of activity and anyone in tune with our world can feel it."

The bus arrived. As soon as Trinity stepped off the bus she almost passed out. She lost her balance and Sam caught her.

"You okay?" he asked, scared.

"It's heavy here," she said, trying to acclimate her breathing.

"Heavy?" Sam asked.

Nicholas nodded.

"I feel it too."

"I didn't realize you would be so sensitive to the presence," Sam commented. "What do you feel?"

She closed her eyes. She drew a deep breath.

"Lots of you."

"Me?"

"Angels."

"You see them, or feel them?"

"Feel," she answered. "But something else."

"What?" Sam quizzed, very curious of Trinity's abilities.

"It's hard to explain."

She took another deep breath.

"I know Logan told me something was coming and it was going to happen here at Stonehenge, but…"

"Something is coming," Nicholas said, matter-of-fact.

"Ya," she said. "It feels like there is a heavy weight in the sky sitting on a bubble. At any moment that weight is going to burst through the bubble. I feel the weight, the anxiety, the evil."

"You feel all that?" Sam asked, wide-eyed.

Trinity grinned and tilted her head to the right.

Sam thought she looked cute.

"Wipe that thought from your head, Sam," he thought to himself.

The three walked through the parking lot. An old woman, dressed like a Romani gypsy sat on a stool along the split rail fence. She was smoking a crude pipe and watching them from beneath her head scarf.

Sam gave her a smile. She nodded. Trinity noticed.

They walked out to the rock formation. All over the surrounding countryside there were thousands of burial mounds. Every field hosted numerous piles of dirt covered by grass. Each mound was about twelve feet by twelve feet and ten or eleven feet high. Nobody really knew what they were for or where they came from.

There were the usual tourists walking around the Stonehenge circle. Trinity found a dry patch of grass and sat down, legs crossed, chin in hands. The boys sat next on either side of her.

"Amazing," she said.

"I know," Nicholas responded.

"What?" Sam asked.

"You think…"

"Ya."

"I hope…"

"I know."

"All this time…"

"I know."

"Wow."

"Ya."

Silence.

Sam stared in bewilderment at the twins' verbal exchange.

Trinity looked at Nicholas.

He nodded and grunted.

"For crying out loud...what are you two talking about?" Sam blurted out.

She grinned.

Nicholas burst out laughing.

Sam shook his head astonished.

"Twins."

"Yup."

Trinity noticed the old woman they had seen by the split rail fence wander near them. She squatted in the grass about 30 feet away, smoking her pipe and pretending to contemplate the stone structure.

"Who is she?" Trinity asked Sam.

He looked at Trinity.

"Logan will tell you when it's time."

She rolled her eyes.

"Oh come on pal Sammy."

"Sam."

"Pal Sam. We're here now. She's here now. Who is she?" she pried, playfully.

"Nope."

"Aw...pwetty pwetty please," Trinity cooed putting her head on his shoulder.

He laughed.

"Sorry girl pal, I can't tell you."

She playfully nudged him with her shoulder and pouted.

He regained his posture and chuckled. It was tempting.

Pleasant silence.

"So what do you think is going to happen here?" she asked Sam.

"I don't know."

"Seriously?"

"This isn't my area of expertise if you know what I mean. I'm not a warrior, I'm a Protector."

"So does that mean you couldn't fight if needed?" she asked.

Wry grin.

"Of course I can fight. I am a Protector …it's what we do. But I'm not assigned to fight in battles. I'm assigned to protect individuals from specific evil forces."

"Warrior on a smaller scale," Nicholas offered.

"Exactly. More like a body guard," Sam explained with a proud smile, his dimples showing. She had never noticed them before. They were cute.

They sat there observing the tourists and taking in the experience. When they were done they loaded back on the bus. As they pulled away from the parking lot Trinity saw the old woman once again sitting on her stool by the fence, watching her.

The gypsy woman acknowledged Trinity with a slight nod. Trinity just stared back.

Nicholas was sitting on the bus, next to a girl his own age and chatted with her while Sam and Trinity sat in silence. When they boarded the train, Nicholas went to find the cute girl he had sat by on the bus.

"What you thinking about?" Sam asked quietly, his head leaned back in the seat. She looked over at him and smiled, then went back to her thoughts.

He leaned in close.

"I can't read your thoughts."

She smirked.

Sigh.

"I've been ripped open by a demon. I've almost died. And I have the feeling that was not the worst moment of my life," she gave him a small, worried smile.

Sam swallowed hard. Everything in him screamed to protect her. She was different. She was special. His protective juices started flowing.

He turned her face toward him.

"I will protect you."

Small, unbelieving smile.

"Against a thousand demons flying through that portal?"

"If I must," Sam assured.

She chuckled.

"Well aren't you the modern day Superman?" she teased.

"It's my job. Minus the red cape and blue tights."

They both laughed.

Later that night Trinity and Sam sat at a little café. Trinity found their friendship very playful. It was enjoyable, much like her and Nicholas' relationship. After a while they walked back to the townhouse. They stopped and sat on the steps watching some kids play in the street.

"Who was the woman?" Trinity asked.

Sam squirmed.

"Come on, I'm going to find out at some point. Why not right now?"

Sam caved.

"The woman at Stonehenge with the pipe is a Guardian."

"An angel?" she asked.

"No. A human Guardian," he explained. "Since Stonehenge was first formed almost at the beginning of the human race, there have been human Guardians that have helped angels keep the portal closed. They fought in the original battle when the portal opened and since then the Guardians have watched the portal."

"So they are mortal…human," she confirmed.

"Yes."

"So, do they just pass the job down from generation to generation, or how does it work?"

"Exactly. It is a job that is passed from generation to generation."

Trinity mused.

"So do they know something is coming?"

"Yes."

"That lady knows who you were?" Trinity asked.

"Yes."

"So she recognizes angels?"

"Yes."

"She recognizes me?"

Silence.

Raised eyebrows.

"Well?" she pressed.

He shrugged.

"You silly angels with your secrets."

He playfully poked her cheek.

She blushed, then grinned.

Chapter Eleven

Sam and Trinity headed to the outdoor market at Covent. They moseyed through all the booths. Trinity found a booth with old compasses and bought one.

"What you need that for?" Sam asked, with a grin.

"It's not for me. It's for you, just in case you get lost."

"Really," he smirked.

"Nope."

Chuckle.

This was by far the best job he'd ever had. Protecting Trinity was fun. She was cute, playful and sarcastic.

"Samuel! Snap out of it!" he chided himself. He could not let himself even think like that. This was an assignment. He must be professional.

"Oh! Look at these!" Trinity grabbed his hand and yanked him towards another booth. Her touch sent tingles through his body. She let go of his hand to grab a leather journal, hand-made with intricate and unique designs.

"These are cool," he said, snapping back to reality. He found one with wings on it and bought it.

"Here, this is for you," he handed her the journal.

Trinity grinned.

"Wait!" He grabbed a pen from the table and wrote on the inside cover.

"I'm always here: to guide and protect you. Samuel."

Trinity grinned.

"Thanks," she said softly.

"Don't forget about me," he said, with a silly grin.

She smirked.

"I know five of your kind and you think I'm going to forget about you?"

"Well, by the end of the summer you may know a lot more," he joked.

"Wait! What?"

"Oops."

He should not have said that.

"Sam?" she said, in a warning voice.

She grabbed his hand, dragged him out of the market to the square and sat him down on the curb.

"Explain," she demanded.

He gave an awkward, sheepish grin.

"Sam you look like someone has duct-taped your smile. What did you mean 'by the end of the summer I might know a lot more' angels?"

Silence.

Sam just stared at her pretty face, mesmerized.

Her shoulder leaned against his.

"It's my life. Tell me," she pleaded.

He sighed.

"I can't."

"Sammy," she whined, and linked her arm around his, leaning her head on his shoulder.

He grinned.

"Come on Sammy, what's it gonna change?"

"I don't know. But I'm not supposed to be telling you possible futures," Sam explained.

She sighed and playfully pushed him with her shoulder.

"Jackass."

He laughed.

"Come on," Trinity stood and pulled him up. "Let's get some food."

The twosome headed toward Trafalgar Square to grab some lunch. They chose something to-go.

"Come, we are going to have lunch with the queen," Sam insisted. He grabbed her hand and they ran to catch the bus.

"What do you mean we are having lunch with the queen?" Trinity asked as they got off the bus in front of Buckingham Palace.

"You know the queen?" she asked, confused.

Sam just grinned as he dragged her to the Victoria Memorial Statue in front of the palace gates. People were camped out eating lunch.

"Here." He plopped down, dragging her with him.

"Lunch with the queen?" Trinity mused.

"She's in there. We're out here. So ya…lunch with the queen," he smirked.

They both laughed.

"Well since this is as close as I'm going to get to the Queen, this will have to do," Trinity said.

"Don't be so sure about that," Sam said.

"Are you kidding me?" Trinity asked, wide-eyed.

"Yes."

She punched him in the arm.

"Ow!" he said rolling up his sleeve.

"Oh did I hurt you?" Trinity asked, concerned.

Sam flexed his bicep.

"No I think I'm good," he grinned, cocky.

Trinity blushed, traced the bulge of his bicep with her finger.

"Ya, you're good."

Chapter Twelve

When Trinity woke up she found another red rose by her bed. She stared at it confused. She was flattered by the secret admirer, but she was worried about how they were getting a rose next to her bed while she slept. She looked at the note left with it.

"Hi," was all it said.

"Sam, are you leaving the roses by my bed," she asked him. He looked at her confused.

"Did you get another one?" he asked.

"Yes."

"Hmmm, I wonder how they are getting them in your room?" he asked, truly confused.

"Do you think it's a good thing or a bad thing?" she asked.

"I don't know. Who do you know that would leave you roses?" he asked.

"Logan, I guess."

"Is that something he has done before?" he asked.

"No," she said. "In fact, he would more likely leave a black feather."

Sam shrugged.

"Do you think its Roan?" she asked.

"Is that something he has done in the past?"

"No."

Sam shrugged.

Trinity and Sam headed out after breakfast. They were going to visit University of Oxford. Trinity was interested in checking them out because she knew the Lacrosse scouts would be courting her this season.

"You don't have to come with me," she said to Sam.

"Ya I do. And it's either in person or incognito."

"Incognito?" she asked, playfully.

"Invisible hovering."

"Ya I'll take in person," she said. "That way I can do this…"
She poked his dimple.

He grabbed her around the shoulders, folding her at the waist and mussed up her hair. She ripped away playfully.

"Hey. It took me all of five long minutes to do my hair," she teased.

"Ya and somehow it always looks great!"

"Hey!" She did not know if that was a compliment or a dig.

"What time did you say the train was at?" Sam asked, distracted.

"Ten-twenty, it is only nine-forty; we have plenty of time to get to the platform."

"Um….the train leaves at nine-fifty," he said, slightly panicked.

"What?" she asked, startled.

"Train's been moved to nine-fifty. We need to run if we want to catch this train."

He grabbed her hand and yanked. The two of them started running down the long tile hallway to find the platform. They wormed through the tunnels, across the sky bridge and got stopped at the escalators. Everybody was quietly waiting their turn to go up them. Trinity stood behind Sam quietly on the escalator breathing heavily from the run. She leaned her forehead against his back.

"I hope we make this."

As soon as they reached the stop they jumped and bolted around people. Sam almost lost Trinity. He grabbed her hand again, pulling her along with him. They shimmied against the wall to get past a group of day-care kids and ran as fast as they could to the platform.

They reached the platform just as they were making the last call. Out of breath and exhausted they handed their tickets to the conductor and plopped down in two chairs on the train.

Laughter.

Once the two gained their composure they looked at each other and burst out laughing, again.

Sam realized he was still holding her hand and let go quickly. Trinity looked at him, eyebrow raised.

"For a minute there I thought I was going to have to break out the wings," he joked, trying to take the attention off his embarrassment.

Just as Trinity looked up, a guy walked by the two of them and turned away. Trinity gasped. She was sure it was Roan: the demon that had tried to seduce her last year and then tried to kill her by slicing open her abdomen.

She stood, facing the back of the guy as he walked into the next car.

"Roan!" she called out. But he was gone.

Trinity bolted to the end of the car to follow him. Samuel followed behind her, suddenly all business.

She ran into the next car looking around frantically. People began to wonder what was wrong with her.

She rushed past a group of seats as someone grabbed her arm and stopped her. She looked down. Roan was sitting in the aisle seat, gripping onto her arm, smug.

"Roan," she whispered.

Sam was stuck behind a rather large woman who was blocking the isle, in the previous car. He was waiting for her to move her luggage around.

"Sit," Roan crooned and pulled her onto his lap, his arm around her waist.

She quickly slid into the seat next to him, unsure of what to do. It was only a few months ago that this demon had tried to kill her.

"Ah. You aren't holding all that against me?" he sneered.

"What do you think?" she spat.

"Baby, I was doing what I thought needed to be done. And you were doing what you thought needed to be done," he crooned, seductively. "We just had a little lover's quarrel."

"Lover's quarrel?" she almost yelled. "You tried to kill me!" she whispered fiercely. "And we are not girlfriend and boyfriend."

He placed his hand on her leg.

"Still don't feel anything?" he asked.

When a demon touches a mortal, that human usually is overcome by the evil, in Roan's case lust, but Trinity was immune to their touch. Roan had always been bothered that Trinity was not affected the way other mortals were.

"No," she said, as she brushed his hand off her leg.

"Still feisty I see," he crooned, with a smirk.

"What are you doing here?" she demanded.

He motioned for her to lean forward so he could whisper to her. She leaned forward, leery. He grabbed the back of her head and kissed her hard. It startled her. The kiss was passionate, yet cold and sent icy tingles down to her toes. It took her a moment to regain her senses. Then she tore herself from his grasp.

He laughed, cruelly.

"I am here for you, Pet."

"You can't have me."

"Trinity let's go!" Sam said, sternly.

She just now noticed him standing there. He had made his way past the large woman with the suitcase. He held out his hand. She took it.

"Oh, looky what we have here," Roan said, mocking. "Trinity has her own Protector." He chuckled. "What? Logan out of the picture now?"

Trinity bristled. She did not know what to say. She wanted to defend Logan, but she did not want to offend Sam.

"I'm here in Logan's stead," Sam interjected, with confidence.

Trinity had never seen this side of Sam. He was strong and in charge of the situation. He put his arm protectively around her waist as he spoke

"Leave her alone Roan...or you know what I will do to you."

Fear flashed across Roan's face and he shrunk into his seat.

Sam led Trinity back to their seats in the other car.

Trinity had lost her breath. Sam, her "Sammy" had always been playful. She had just seen what he was really here for. To protect her.

They sat in silence.

She had mixed emotions. Excited. Swooned. Unsure. Confused. She just wanted to return to the casual friendship they had just minutes before.

The train pulled up to the station and the two got off in silence. Trinity looked around for Roan but knew she would not see him.

Sam and Trinity checked in at the University of Oxford visitor center to get their passes. They had a guide who showed them around the campus. Trinity asked a lot of questions. She loved the architecture. Oxford was the oldest university in England. She grew excited at the prospect of spending four years here.

Sam liked to watch Trinity when she was excited. Her face lit up and her eyes sparkled. She was like a little kid on Christmas morning. It made him feel warm and fuzzy.

The two left the guide and headed to the cafeteria. They got lunch and sat on one of the large lawns where students were sprawled out eating and doing homework.

Trinity plopped down, legs crossed. Sam sat beside her.

"I like it here."

Those were the first words she had said to him since the train.

"I can tell," he smiled.

She looked at him sideways and grinned.

"That obvious?"

"Oh ya."

"I'll have to work on that. Don't want to let the scouts know how much I want to go to school here," she said.

"Game face."

"Exactly."

Silence.

"What's Roan doing here?" she asked, looking out over the campus. She was afraid to look at Sam.

"What did he say to you?"

She looked at Sam, paused, then looked away.

67

"He's here for me."

Sam just nodded, knowing.

"Why? Why again?"

Sam looked at Trinity, who was staring… off into the distance. He took her chin into his hand and turned her face towards him.

"You are important. You are very, very important," he said, softly.

She frowned.

"How?"

He grinned and dropped his hand from her chin.

"I can't tell you."

"Oh!" she groaned and mussed up his hair.

"I surrender. I surrender," he joked rolling away from her onto his stomach to protect himself.

She lay on her stomach next to him and propped herself up with her arms.

"You're gonna tell me," she stated, matter-of-fact.

"Nope.

"Fine. So much for being my Pal Sammy," she said, miffed.

"It's Sam."

"Sammy."

"Samuel."

"Sammy," she insisted, smugly.

He rolled his eyes and pushed her shoulder with his.

She pulled at the grass.

Silence.

"Is he going to try to kill me?" she asked softly.

Sam looked at her, then at the grass.

"Hmmm?" she probed, looking at him.

He looked up at her.

"Maybe. Or turn you," he answered.

"He's tried both, and failed," she said.

"Roan's not a quitter."

"Great."

Sarcasm.

Sam poked her cheek.

"Cheer up, Teacup. I will protect you."

Butterflies tickled her stomach. After watching how he dealt with Roan on the train, she knew he could.

"Hi," he said.

"Hi," she said.

Somehow that made her feel better.

Chapter Thirteen

Trinity packed her clothes and her guitar. She was taking the train to Paris with Sam, Nicholas, Alaina and her band. The next part of the singing competition was in Paris this weekend. Logan was not back so would not be going with them. But she was happy Sam was here with her.

"Trinity, you ready?" Nicholas yelled up the stairs.

She ran down the stairs with her duffle bag.

"Right here," she smirked.

"We only waited for like twenty minutes," he teased.

"I had to spend more time on my hair since Sam thinks five minutes is inadequate," she said.

Sam reach his hand out and mussed up her hair.

"There! Looks great!" he said with satisfaction.

She pushed his hand away, exasperated.

Nicholas watched, amused. "I see we are getting along famously."

"Oh ya. Just great," she mocked, trying to comb her hair with her fingers.

"Never better. You coming, Teacup?" Sam said as he marched towards the front door.

"I'm not a Teacup, Sammy!" Trinity scolded.

"And I'm not Sammy, and yet...."

"Touché."

Out the door they went.

The three met Alaina when they got to the train station. Hugs all around.

"Why couldn't Logan come?" Trinity asked, glancing at Sam.

"Still busy."

Trinity knew he would be here if he could. They rode the bullet train under the channel to Paris. She had never been to Paris and was excited to see the Eiffel Tower. She could not believe the stage for the competition would be set up right below the Eiffel Tower. At night the tower sparkled every hour for several minutes.

Alaina and Nicholas went to the food car to see if they could round up some breakfast. Sam and Trinity sat in silence.

"You upset Logan couldn't come?" Sam asked.

"Sorta."

"Sorry I had to be here instead."

"Oh no!" Trinity apologized, concerned. "I want you here. I just wish….."

"…he was here too," Sam finished for her.

Trinity felt awkward.

"It's okay. We're both your friends," Sam played it off casually.

Silence.

Trinity watched out the window and listened to the movement of the train on the tracks.

Sam poked her cheek.

"Hey…"

She smiled and looked over at him.

"What, Sammy?"

He playfully grimaced. "What ya thinking about?"

"Everything."

She gave a painful smile.

"Uh oh. That wasn't a good smile," he observed out loud.

She sighed.

He brushed shoulders with her and leaned close.

"Talk to me."

"It's everything jumbled up into one big hot mess. The excitement of the competition, the nervousness of running into Roan again. Stonehenge and what's going to happen. The unknown of something evil ahead. Logan. You…." Her voice trailed off.

"It's a lot to deal with, I know," he assured her. "I'm here. I'm not leaving your side."

She smirked. "But you're so cute and cuddly. It's hard to picture you destroying Roan."

It was his turn to smirk. He turned away from her and muttered, "We'll see."

Trinity trembled at his confidence. Then she remembered back to the previous train ride where he threatened Roan. She had never seen Roan afraid before, but he was definitely afraid of Samuel. She blushed.

They rode in silence. Alaina and Nicholas came back from the food car with an arm full of goodies. They ate and chatted about Trinity's upcoming concert.

The train arrived and they shared a taxi to their hotel. They were staying right near the Eiffel tower. They unloaded their gear and made their way to the venue to see if Trinity had a dress rehearsal.

As they rounded the corner, there stood the Eiffel Tower. The stage was all set up, the Tower in the background. It was going to be so epic. Trinity checked in and they told her tomorrow afternoon she would have a quick run-through and then she was playing last in the performance. She was suddenly nervous. Sam sensed her change in her mood and gave her hand a secret squeeze. His assurance calmed her.

"So what do we want to do today? We have all day and night before the performance," Nicholas said.

"Let's go up the Eiffel Tower tonight," Trinity suggested. "What about going to the Louvre today?"

"Yes!" Nicholas exclaimed. "I've always wanted to go see the Louvre."

So the foursome walk down the stairs to take the subway to the museum. When they were walking through the underground subway halls, they heard a beautiful violin. As they approached they saw a woman playing her violin, the case open on the ground with a few euro tossed inside by passersby. They stopped to listen. The music swelled around them. The halls had amazing acoustics.

Sam grabbed Trinity and led her in a waltz. She giggled. Alaina and Nicholas smiled. Soon Nicholas bowed and offered his hand to Alaina and they were off dancing. People stopped to watch. An elderly French couple joined in and danced beside them. People put more coins in the violin case.

Trinity felt warm and secure in Sam's arms. As she swirled around, she giggled and held tight to Sam. She loved that he made her laugh. Toward the end of the song, they slowed their dance. Sam felt the urge to kiss her. But he dare not.

They stood in each other's arms awkwardly, neither wanting to let go. But when the music stopped they released their embrace.

Once in the Louvre, the four decided to focus on one section. It is said that if you spend thirty seconds on each piece, and saw every piece in the Louvre, it would take you a hundred days to see everything.

They saw paintings that the twins had studied in school. Sam walked with Trinity. He wanted to hold her hand. But he knew he could not, he should not.

"How can I have feelings for a human?" he asked himself.

He had never fallen for a human. Sure, he had been friends with many humans, but nothing like this. He wondered if this was why Logan wanted him to protect Trinity while he was away, because he cared for her with this kind of intensity.

There was something about Trinity that was magnetic.

After the Louvre they stopped at a little market and purchased salami, olives, and several cheeses. When they passed a bakery they bought a fresh loaf of French bread. They ate dinner in the soft grass beneath the Eiffel Tower. It was just like a storybook. Magical.

Trinity had a twinge of regret that she was enjoying herself with Sam while Logan was not here. But she told herself that it wasn't her fault that Logan was still gone.

Alaina and Nicholas headed back to the hotel and Sam and Trinity stood in line to go up to the top of the Eiffel Tower.

They stood in silence.

Sam poked her cheek.

"Hi," he said.

"Hi?" she asked. "After thousands of years, all you can come up with is 'Hi'?"

He shrugged.

She smiled.

They bought their tickets and got on the lift. They had a window spot. Everyone was packed in tightly, and Trinity was getting jostled around. Sam put his arm around her shoulder to hold her steady. She loved the view. The lift took them up inside the Eiffel to the third level, the highest level that visitors could get to.

She could feel Sam's breath on her neck. It sent tingles down her back. She felt guilty.

"What do you think?" he asked, looking out the window.

"It's breathtaking."

"Yes it is," he said, looking at her, not the view.

She looked back at him, her heart skipped a beat. Then she frowned.

"You ready for tomorrow?" he asked suddenly.

She nodded.

"How many songs do you get to sing?"

"Just one. But if I get in the top five, there is a final concert at Stonehenge where I sing three songs," she said.

"Stonehenge?" he asked, in disbelief.

"Ya," she said looking back at him, knowing what he was thinking.

He just stared at her.

She stared back and nodded.

It was not a coincidence. Everything was orchestrated to have her at Stonehenge for the final concert just as an entire flight of demons were trying to break through the portal.

Sam tensed.

"You better not get nervous too," she said, smartly. "You're the big bad protector angel, remember? It's my job to be scared."

He laughed and loosened up.

"I'm not scared."

"No? But concerned."

He smirked.

"I got this."

"Ah ya I forgot…Superman without the cape right?"

"And no tights," Sam insisted.

She giggled.

"Exactly."

Chapter Fourteen

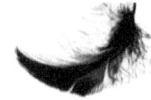

The view from the top of the Eiffel tower was amazing. The sky was dark, the Tower was lit below them and in ten minutes it would sparkle, lighting the night. Sam and Trinity walked along the entire edge of the view deck, the fresh summer air brushing her hair back.

She leaned on the railing and looked out. Sam stood by her.

"I'm sure this isn't anything special to you," she said. "You've probably been up here many times."

"No. This is my first actually," he admitted.

"Really?" she mused. "You've been around for thousands of years and this is your first time?

He nodded. Pleased.

"Glad I could be here with you," she said.

"Me too." He gave her a little nudge with his shoulder.

She grinned. She looked out over the city.

"Seems so peaceful and perfect from up here," she said.

"Ya it does," he leaned in closer.

"Wish everything was always like this. Perfect. Quiet. In harmony."

He chuckled.

"It's earth. It's complicated and messy. But it's wonderful!"

She looked into his crystal blue eyes. His blonde curly hair ruffled in the breeze. She wanted him to kiss her. He wanted to kiss her. But it was such a bad idea.

Instead he leaned in and whispered.

"You are the most amazing human I have ever met."

Their cheeks brushed. She gasped slightly.

"Well look what we have here?" she heard a wicked voice say.

Trinity whipped around and faced Roan.

"What are you doing here?" she spat.

"I told you," he sneered.

"I'm not going with you," she said.

"Roan!" Sam said, sternly.

"Samuel," Roan said, acknowledging his presence. "You going to be by her side every second?"

"Every second," he confirmed.

Roan sighed.

"Well I wasn't expecting you Samuel. This definitely puts a kink in my plans. But then again, I don't mind kink."

Sam stood ready. He was all business. His change in demeanor went from cute, cuddly Sam to, well…Protector.

"I'm going to put more than a kink in your plans if you come near Trinity."

Roan chuckled, but backed up a step.

"Okay, okay. Don't get so pushy Samuel. I hear ya."

"I'll catch you another time, Pet," Roan crooned, and winked at Trinity.

Next thing she knew, he was gone. She looked at Sam.

"He's scared of you, isn't he?" she asked in amazement.

Sam just grinned.

"You some legendary fighter or something?"

He just continued to grin.

"When do I get to see this legendary Sammy?" she asked.

He shrugged.

Silence.

"Hi," he said, grinning.

She smiled.

"Hi."

Chapter Fifteen

Trinity was at the top of the Eiffel Tower by herself. Sam was nowhere to be found. She was confused. He had just been here a moment ago. She looked over the edge and saw thousands of little creatures scurrying up the legs of the Eiffel tower. They were black, bat-like, with spindly legs, leathery skin and beady black eyes. She closed her eyes and opened them again. The creatures were still coming.

Trinity backed up. She did not know what was going on. Once again she leaned over the edge and as the creatures got closer she could see their sharp, pointed teeth and saliva drooling from the sides of their mouths. Her heart pounded in her chest, her hands became clammy. Trinity was scared.

As they scurried closer she could hear their toxic whispers, the screeching in glee, as they reached the top and began to pour over the edge. She screamed. The creatures leapt off the edge at her. A pair of strong arms grabbed her, encompassed her and shielded her from the demons. The creatures bounced off him.

She did not know who protected her. She assumed it was Sam.

"Back!" she heard an authoritative voice.

Startled, she looked up into the face of her protector. Roan.

He had his arms wrapped around her and grinned down at her lasciviously.

"I can protect you," he assured her. "These fiends must listen to me."

She pushed him away.

"You are one of them," she said, unsure how far she should back away.

The little demons swarmed around, waiting to attack.

"I am their master. They can't hurt you while you are with me."

Trinity was unsure. Roan was evil. He had tried to kill her. But right now he was all that stood between her and the evil spirits tearing her apart.

"Come to me," he whispered. "Come to me."

He reached out his hand to her.

Trinity jolted awake. She sat up, sweating in the dark. It had all been a dream and she was safe in her bed in the hotel. Sigh of relief. She flopped down on her bed, her heart still racing, and closed her eyes.

She felt a hand on her arm.

"It's okay. It's just a dream."

She bolted straight up and in one motion stood on her bed with her back to the walls. Roan was standing beside her bed. This time it was real.

Roan cackled.

"Startle much?" he asked.

She stood awkwardly on her bed. He stood beside it, not three feet away.

"I'm not going to hurt you," he said, softly.

Trinity pressed her back further against the wall.

"I'm here to protect you," he cooed.

"Sam is here to protect me," she said, matter-of-factly.

"He can't stop all those demons, but I can," he said.

She glared.

"Go back to sleep. I'll watch over you," he promised.

"Sam, please come and protect me. Roan is here. I need you. Please come protect me," she prayed, silently.

She knew Sam would hear her prayers.

A look of terror flashed across Roan's face.

The bedroom door flew open. Sam charged Roan, throwing him hard against the wall. He was glowing. Shirtless, he had a sword slung across his back, ready for battle. He was magnificent. Trinity backed up away, off the bed, staying close to the wall.

With one hand Sam held Roan against the wall. Roan's feet dangled uselessly.

"Roan, get out!" Sam commanded. "And stay out."

83

Roan had fear in his eyes. He shrank away until he completely disappeared.

Instantly "Protector Angel Samuel" transitioned back to "cute and cuddly Sammy." He stood in his worn pajama pants, no glow, no sword. Just Sam.

"You okay? He asked, gently, coming over to Trinity.

She nodded. Mouth agape.

Sammy really was a super-hero. No cape or tights needed. Even powerful demons like Roan cowered at his mere presence. Trinity almost swooned. She had seen Logan fight in all of his glory, but Sam had passion when he fought. And there was something magnificent and compelling about that passion.

He helped her back into her bed. She was trembling. The bad dream, Roan's presence in her room, it was all deeply disturbing. Sam tucked her. Tenderly, as if she was a child.

"I won't leave you alone tonight," he assured her. "I'll stand watch in the doorway."

She closed her eyes. "Night night Sammy."

Trinity slept peacefully the rest of the night.

Chapter Sixteen

The next day Trinity was refreshed and ready for the competition. She spent the afternoon with her band making small changes here and there. She knew Sam was near even though she could not see him. She was pretty sure he was using his ability to be present but not seen. She could feel him. Near. Even next to her. She sighed every time she felt his presence.

She was sitting on a speaker box rewriting a lyric when she felt Sam's presence. No one else was around.

"I can feel you," she whispered.

Silence.

"You don't have to hide all the time. You could actually be here with me," she stated, in a sassy voice.

85

She knew Sam was enjoying it. She felt a brush of something against her arm, he was not physically there but she knew it was him, making his presence known.

"Fine. Be all invisible and mysterious," she said, resigned.

Nicholas and Alaina were somewhere in the crowd beneath the Eiffel Tower. The time was drawing near for her to perform. She knew Sam was still with her. She could sense when he came and went.

Darkness began to fall as the competition began. Trinity and her band sat backstage listening to the competition play. Some of them were really good. Others, not so much. She needed to place in the top five to make it to the final competition, an epic concert at Stonehenge.

Tonight she wore a red tulle dress and corset and her black and gray striped thigh-highs and combat boots, of course. Her long black hair was held back with a red ribbon. Her hair curled and waved down her back. It was unruly, yet "put together" all at the same time. She had her black guitar with her tonight.

Trinity got nervous as it neared her turn. She only got to sing one song, a new one she had written this summer. She looked at her black painted nails and wished she had touched them up. She bit her red lip.

"Don't be nervous," she heard Sam whisper. She turned and he was there right behind her, leaning over her shoulder.

"I'm trying," she said.

"You've got this. You are the best here," he assured her.

She smiled and nodded. He gave her a big hug. Then he was gone. She felt better.

Trinity appeared on stage with her band. The crowd cheered. She was pumped. She could do this.

The crowd silenced as the spotlight shown on Trinity. Her haunting voice filled the air. A capella, no music at first. The crowd was entranced. Then piano began to accompany her. All the stage lights strobe as the band rocked; guitar, drums, bass. The song took flight. The crowd went wild. Trinity was in her element. She slung the guitar around to her back and strutted across the stage, singing with intensity. Trinity's own brand of gothic rock, kind of like Evanescence but not quite. The audience was eating out of her hand. She knew she would move onto the competition at Stonehenge. It was destiny.

The song ended. The crowd screamed. Trinity bowed. She made the top five. Elation.

Chapter Seventeen

That night Trinity could not sleep. She bounced off the walls. She jumped on the couch. She was so excited. Her brother, Alaina and Sam all thought she was crazy. She had a natural high and could not help the excitement she felt at having made it this far in the competition.

"How much caffeine have you had to drink?" Sam asked, watching her jump up and down on the couch.

"None."

"Yikes!"

"I'm just excited," she assured him, still jumping up and down.

"Guys I'm going to bed. I'll see you in the morning. Let's grab some croissants before we visit Notre Dame," Nicholas said.

Alaina went to bed as well.

Sam and Trinity were left together. She plopped down from her feet to her knees on the couch. She leaned forward towards Sam like a little kid.

"We were the best weren't we?" she asked, excited.

He nodded, smiling.

"I knew it!" she said with glee and jumped up to bounce up and down on the couch again.

Sam laughed at her childish energy.

Sam eyed her mischievously. Then quickly reached out, grabbed her foot and pulled it out from under her. She lost her balance and crashed down onto the pillows. They laughed. She sat up and pushed him off the couch.

A little surprised, Sam stood up, grabbed a pillow and smacked her with it. Trinity giggled, grabbed several pillows and began lobbing them at him. Her accuracy caught him off guard. But now he had all the pillows. She stared at him wide-eyed, playfully frightened.

"You are doomed," he laughed.

She jumped off the couch and froze; ready to dive out of the way of a flying pillow. He stood posed, ready to strike, a pillow in each hand. Suddenly she dived across the couch and tackled him. He was startled by the move. She tore all the pillows from his grasp and scurried to the other side of the couch. Now she had all the pillows.

"Well played, Teacup," he said, surprised.

"Thanks, Sammy," she said.

They stood staring, smiling.

She launched one pillow to make him duck and pin him down, then she launched the others to his huddled position. She kept one, leapt over the couch and started beating him with it.

"I surrender. I surrender," he said, lifting his arm.

"How macho of you," she teased.

"Hey I'll take on demons any day, but Trinity with pillows is far more dangerous," he chuckled.

She stood with the pillow ready to strike again.

"How so?" she laughed.

He stood up straight, face-to-face with her. His breath hot on her forehead. She dropped her pillow and trembled.

He looked at her red lips. His arms ached to hold her. She bit her lip, and his lips quivered in response.

"Don't do that," he begged.

She stopped. Wide-eyed. Questioning.

"You are dangerous, because you are more tempting than anything I've ever faced. You are more tempting than The Fall," he whispered.

"Do I have feelings for him?" she asked, not realizing she said it out loud.

"Was that a question or a statement?" he asked, also confused.

"I don't know. I'm so confused," she whispered.

"Me too."

Painful silence.

She squeezed her eyes closed and realized she could not do this. Not with Logan still thinking she cared for him. And she did care for him. In fact she thought she loved him. But how can she care for Sam and Logan so intensely at the same time?

She needed to see Logan. She needed to get her head right.

She backed away slowly.

"I can't," she said, quietly.

"I know."

He walked her to her bedroom silently. She climbed in bed and pulled the covers up.

"I'll be right outside the door," he said. If you have a bad dream or Roan comes back you call for me."

She nodded.

He leaned down and brushed the hair away from her face.

"You are a beautiful creature."

She flushed and replied, "You are too."

Now Sam flushed.

"Night night Sammy."

He left, but only as far as the door, where he waited all night.

Notre Dame Cathedral. It was dark and dreary, like a poem by Edgar Allen Poe. Trinity knew she was dreaming but she wanted to see what happened, so she didn't stop the dream. She climbed the stairs to the top of the church. The gargoyles overhead. The sky clouded and rain began to fall. Lightning crashed around her and thunder shook the stone steps. She stood, drenched to the skin in her white, tulle dress with a black ribbon sash around her waist. Her black and white striped socks were scrunched up wet near her ankle-high combat boots. She stood in the rain, waiting, watching.

As she examined one of the gargoyles she noticed it slowly changed shape. The face morphed to that of Roan's and its demon body moved toward her. She froze. The demon body changed to Roan's human form as he drew near. She remained frozen.

"Demons are coming," he whispered.

She stared at him.

"I will protect you," he assured her. "I control them."

"Sam will protect me," she said.

"He can't protect you from these demons," Roan warned.

Roan grabbed her arm and pulled her close to him. He leered into her face.

"Come with me." His hot breath smelled like smoke.

"No," she said, simply. Unafraid.

He grinned. He lifted her roughly and threw her over his shoulders. He jumped from the church balcony down to the ground. The distance was hundreds of feet. The leap was nothing short of supernatural. He carried her swiftly down a dark alley. She could not see anything.

Trinity bolted awake.

Chapter Eighteen

The next morning Trinity awoke and there was a red rose next to her bed. A small note read simply, "Congratulations."

Trinity shot out of bed, rose in hand. She stood in the middle of the room staring at it. Wondering. This was the third red rose she had received. She lifted it to her nose. It smelled sweet. She smiled inside. It was nice to have a secret admirer. She just hoped with all her heart it was not from Roan.

Later, the four were having espresso and crepes on the Rue Cler. A group of girls walked by and spotted Trinity. They squealed.

"Oh my gosh it's that girl!"

They ran over and asked Trinity for her autograph. She was flattered and shyly smiled as she signed her autograph. She grinned at her brother, embarrassed.

"That's so cool," Nicholas said.

Trinity shrugged. She did not know if she thought it was or not.

They continued to watch life go by as they ate. Trinity rocked a black tulle skirt, a black and white off-the-shoulder striped shirt and shredded tights. Her final statement was a pair of red combat boots. She shook her unruly hair.

They took the metro to Notre Dame. Trinity was nervous. Her dream last night had her on edge. Roan had kidnapped her at this very spot in her dream. Since her dreams had a tendency to come true, she was nervous this morning.

As they approached the cathedral from the other side of the river, they saw vendors with art and little knick-knacks for sale. They perused the booths. Trinity bought a few trinkets and shoved them in her little backpack.

They stood in line to go into the cathedral. The clouds started to roll in. The skies darkened. Trinity stiffened. Exactly like her dream. Sam immediately knew something was wrong. He looked at Trinity. She was nervous. He placed his arm protectively around her shoulders.

"You okay?"

"I had a dream about this."

Raised eyebrow.

"And my dreams often come true, especially when they involve demons," she explained.

"What happened in your dream?" Sam asked.

Trinity did not know if she should tell him. She usually had more than one dream before they came true. But she was here, at Notre Dame, the sky was cloudy. It felt the same.

"I was here, at Notre Dame," she began. "Roan was here too."

Sam squeezed her shoulders, "Nothing is going to happen to you. You have seen how Roan behaves around me. He cowers, he is scared. I will eat him for lunch if he comes near you and he knows it."

"You can't be with me every second," she said.

"I can. I will."

Sam was firm and confident.

They went into the cathedral. It was breath-taking. Everyone was quiet and reverent. Trinity slowly looked at each of the alcoves. The stained glass was marvelous. Trinity lit a candle and said a little prayer. She felt calm. She sighed with relief. It was amazing how a little prayer brought peace, calmness.

Sam waited quietly behind her, giving her privacy. And yet, she knew he could hear her prayers.

"So why are there gargoyles on churches?" she asked Sam, in a hushed voice.

"Actually, a gargoyle is almost like a gutter on a house. The water runs through the gutters, and off the roof of the church through gargoyles' mouths," Sam explained.

"Seriously?"

"Yup."

"But, why do they have to be so ominous?" she asked.

"It was thought during medieval times that gargoyles scared off evil spirits. That they kept demons outside the church."

"Hmmm. Interesting," she said. "I find them odd on a church. But cool at the same time, if that makes any sense."

Everyone wanted to climb to the top of the cathedral where the gargoyles were. Trinity was hesitant but went anyway. Sure enough, it began to rain. Trinity watched the gargoyles warily; she did not want to see any of them move! The other three walked around the corner while Trinity stood watching a gargoyle. She did not notice she was by herself until it was too late.

"Hey, beautiful," Roan crooned in her ear. She had been so preoccupied she did not even hear him come up behind her.

She stiffened.

"Ah, don't stress love. I'm not here to throw you over my shoulder," he whispered. He moved close behind her and leaned his head over her shoulder.

She knew he had seen her dreams before, back during the school year. It did not occur to her that he was still seeing them. But obviously, from that comment, he did see them.

She stood in the rain. Thunder clapped. It was like something straight out of an old black and white horror flick. Standing atop Notre Dame Cathedral, a demon leering dangerously over her. In the rain.

"I only have a second, but I wanted to remind you I am here."

Then he was gone.

Trinity could not understand his infatuation with her. What was it he wanted from her? Why was he promising to take care of her, to protect her from all the other demons? He could not possibly be falling for her. The idea sent shivers down her spine.

"Ready to go, Teacup?" Sam asked.

She nodded.

They made their way down the long staircase. By the time they reached the bottom the rain had stopped and the sun was drying everything around them. Like nothing had happened.

"Perfect timing," Nicholas said. "The sun comes up after we stood in the rain all afternoon."

Nicholas noticed his sister's quiet mood. He walked up, put his arm around her.

"You okay?" he asked.

"Ya."

"Worried?"

"Ya."

Silence.

"I don't know how, but everything is going to be okay," he assured her.

She smiled and leaned her head on his shoulder.

"Wish I was that confident."

"It's easy for me," he said. "I'm not the one having the bad dreams.

"How'd you know?" she asked.

He gave her a look. "Seriously?"

"Ya ya," she mused.

They were twins, they sensed things. They knew each other's moods. They could finish each other's sentences.

"I know Sam's here. But I'm looking out for ya as well," he assured her.

She smiled.

"You have a sword like Sam?" she asked, smartly.

"Working on that."

"Oh ya, with what?"

"Cardboard, tinfoil and duct tape," he answered.

They giggled together. Nicholas gave her a squeeze.

It felt good to laugh.

"Oh wait. I wanted to get a photo of Notre Dame before we leave," she said.

She got her phone out and framed up the shot. She noticed something odd and put her phone down. Up on the top of the cathedral the gargoyles were not stone. They looked dark and leathery. She stared silently trying to focus her eyes. She was sure they were not stone. She was sure they were real demons, perched, waiting, watching.

They turned and looked at her. She put the phone up to take the photo. Snap. When she looked at the photo on her phone, the gargoyles were stone, nothing unusual at all. She looked back at them in real life. Definitely demons.

Chapter Nineteen

Everyone was asleep. It was dark out, almost midnight. Trinity ran down to the little pastry shop on the corner. She wanted a croissant and an espresso. She hated to waken Sam and she knew it was just down the street, so she snuck out. Stupid, she knew, but her coffee craving won over smarts.

As she was rushing back from the pastry shop she ran around a corner and nearly bumped into Roan. She dropped her coffee and pastry bag.

"Sorry beautiful, didn't mean to spill your coffee," he cooed.

"Dang it Roan! Go away."

"I can't do that love."

"What do you want?" she asked, exasperated.

"You know what I want."

"No not really. I know you want me to come with you. But I don't really know what that means and how that is even possible and I'm getting really tired of all this," she rambled.

"I want you to be with me, to come to my side," he explained, in a soothing voice.

"Come on Roan, we both know that's not going to happen," she said, tired.

"You in love with your angel?" he mocked.

She sighed and rolled her eyes.

"Excuse me, are you in love with your angels? Plural," he corrected.

She tried to push past him, her coffee and pastry still on the ground. He did not let her go by. He wrapped his arm around the front of her waist.

"You could love me," he cooed.

She slouched. He was not going to give up. She looked into his eyes.

"I'm not going to love you. You know that," she said.

"You could lust after me," he smirked.

Her shoulders sagged. She was too tired to deal with Roan and his unwanted affections.

"You forget that I've seen the real you. This human shell of yours is fake. Inside you are leathery, ugly," she spat.

He pushed her against the brick wall, leaned into her and kissed her hard. She shivered from head to toe. He would not let up. He was passionate and everything in her cried out for it to stop.

Finally he loosened his lips and looked down at her with an evil grin.

"Come on Pet, I know you liked that."

She glared. Fuming.

"You are a demon," she said. "You are evil."

Roan laughed loudly.

"And your Logan…you think he is good?"

"He is good. Inside he isn't something vicious and ugly like you. He is righteous and radiant," she said, confidently.

She pushed past him and walked toward the hotel.

"Pet, you are strong, beautiful and stubborn."

"Nothing wrong with any of those," she replied, over her shoulder.

"Oh how you make me want you more."

Trinity walked away.

When Trinity got back to the suite Sam was waiting.

"You okay? He asked.

"Fine. Just went out for a pastry and espresso."

"Ah," he said with a raised eyebrow, noticing she did not have either.

She did not know if he knew. She did not know if he had been hovering invisibly over her. But she left it at that.

She washed her face and climbed in bed. Sam followed her.

"You scared at all?" he asked, sitting on the edge of her bed.

"Not really. Tired. Weary. But not scared."

Sam put his hand on her forehead. He leaned over, eyes closed, and whispered.

"May the Lord bless you and protect you and keep you safe through the night. Amen."

He walked toward the door.

"What was that?" she asked, feeling warm and safe.

"A blessing."

She liked it.

He guarded the door all night.

Chapter Twenty

The next morning, there was a knock on the door. Trinity ran to answer it. She opened the door. It was Logan. She screamed and hugged him. He squeezed her tightly. He breathed her in. She smelled like flowers and spices. Human. He realized how much he had missed her.

They walked into the suite hand-in-hand. Nicholas gave Logan a man hug. Sam and Logan nodded at each other. Trinity realized how awkward this was going to be. She did not know how to behave. Logan made it easy. He sat on the couch and pulled Trinity next to him.

"Tell me about the concert," he said.

Trinity told him all the details: what she wore; what she sang; and how amazing it was to be performing at night below a sparkling Eiffel tower.

Logan ran his fingers through Trinity's thick hair and gently pulled her to him. He kissed her. It was small and soft and she felt loved.

Trinity jumped up and told Logan she had to get ready. While she was in the bathroom it occurred to her that Sam might be leaving since Logan was back. She did not want Sam to leave, but she also knew how awkward it would be if he stayed.

When she came out of the bathroom Logan and Sam were talking about it.

"Hey Sam thanks. I'm around for a while. When we need you again, I'll let you know," Logan said.

"Actually, I don't really have another assignment right now and I'd like to stay and make sure Trinity is safe," Sam responded.

"No, I've got it from here," Logan assured him, sternly.

Sam stood still. He understood, but he did not want to obey. Trinity wondered who out-ranked whom in this situation. Probably Logan. The silence was awkward to say the least.

"Samuel, I'd like some time with Trinity, right now," Logan demanded.

Sam turned to Trinity and asked her to walk him out.

"I have to go," he said when they were out of Logan's view.

"I know. It's best for now," Trinity told him.

"You sure?" Sam asked.

Trinity did not want to look him in the eyes.

"I will be watching you, protecting you. Do not fear," he said, assurance and authority lacing the tone of his voice.

"That could get weird you know," she joked.

He chuckled. "I'm a protector, I can't help it."

"I know."

"Well Teacup, I hope this isn't the last moment I get with you."

He poked her cheek.

"Bye Sammy," she whispered.

He did not correct her this time. He smiled.

He left.

After several minutes, Trinity returned upstairs, excited and sad at the same time.

Suddenly, Trinity had a vision. Logan was standing before her dressed as a warrior. He glimmered in the sunlight, a sword in his hand. He was brawny and ready for battle. Then the vision was gone. Trinity still was not sure what these visions were. She stored this one away to ask Logan later.

"So what do you want to do your last day in Paris?" Logan asked.

"I don't know. We've seen so much already," Trinity said.

"You mind if we just have a picnic on the lawn by the Eiffel tower this afternoon?" he asked. "I could use some time with you."

Trinity nodded shyly.

Everyone walked to the market to grab some goodies for a picnic. Nicholas and Alaina ran off to find some cards so they could play games. Logan held Trinity's hand and would not let go. He pulled her close.

"I have missed you so much," he said. "I've missed everything about you, your smell, your smile, your smart mouth."

He laughed.

She grinned.

She was not sure how to act. She had spent so much time with Sam recently and their friendship was completely different. It was playful. She was not sure quite how she fit with Logan anymore. She felt off. It was confusing.

Logan and Trinity plopped down on the grass, the Eiffel Tower looming over them. Logan laid his head in her lap and looked up at her.

"So tell me what's been going on? He asked. "Anything new? Anything different? Anything exciting?"

Trinity suddenly felt relieved. This was Logan, the angel she had gone to battle with, the one she had told everything to, the one that had saved her life. Suddenly everything came pouring out. Each of her encounters with Roan. What he had said. She even told him about the two kisses.

Logan tensed a little but he was not angry with her. It was not her fault and he knew Roan was trying to seduce her to the dark side. She told him everything. He was pleased with her strength and ability to stand up to Roan. Most girls could not. They could not even fight the power of his touch. After all, he was the Demon of Lust.

She told him about her dreams. When she did, Logan sat up. He scooted her close to him. He kept his arm around her.

"You think this dream will come true?" she asked.

Logan looked off into the distance.

"I don't know. But your dreams do have a funny way of coming true, don't they?" he mused.

Trinity nodded and looked away.

Alaina and Nicholas came back with a deck of cards and the four played games all afternoon. Later they all lay on their backs staring at the clouds.

"When we get back to London I'd like to take you to Stonehenge," Logan said.

"We went a few weeks ago. I'd like to go back. I have a lot of questions," Trinity said.

He nodded.

"Miss me?" he asked.

"Sure."

"Sure?"

"Ya. Sure," she teased.

He swatted at her.

"I see leaving Samuel wasn't such a good idea," he quipped.

"I don't know about that," she teased.

"I do," he said, slightly jealous, eyeing her.

"He kept Roan in check," she said, feeling guilty and hoping Logan couldn't see it.

"He and Roan go way back," Logan said.

"What? Explain."

"Nope."

It was her turn to smack him.

"You don't have to tell me, but I know Sammy…" Trinity began.

"Sammy?" Logan said with a funny grin.

"Sorry, Samuel," Trinity corrected. "But I know that he and Roan fought at some point and Sammy…Samuel won."

Logan nodded.

"I mean Roan cowers at Samuel's voice," Trinity continued.

Logan nodded again.

"So what happened?"

Logan shook his head. He was not going to tell.

"Oh come on Logan, what happened?" Trinity pleaded.

"It's not my story to tell," he said looking at her.

She understood. She did not like it, but she understood.

There was a long pause.

Trinity knew she needed to tell Logan about her confused feelings for Sam but she did not know how.

"Logan…" she began.

"Yes," he said looking over at her.

His face was beautiful. He could not be more perfect.

Looking at him she was not confused anymore. But when she looked away, the confusion swept over her like a flood.

They sat in the grass until there it was time to catch the train back to London.

Chapter Twenty-One

Trinity, Nicholas, Alaina and Logan were on the train to Stonehenge. Trinity thought about that last time she had been there. It was with Sam and he had protected her from Roan. She wondered about the gypsy lady and wondered if she was going to get the chance to meet her.

Her brother nudged her. "Here we go again."

"The train or Stonehenge?"

Her brother laughed. "I didn't think about being on a train again. Guess some people would be nervous about taking train rides after they'd been on one that flipped off the track."

Trinity grimaced.

"Nervous?"

"Nope."

"Me either."

"So it's Stonehenge," she said.

"Where all the evil in the world wants to burst through a portal and onto earth."

"How encouraging," she teased.

"Just keeping it real sis."

"Like always."

"Yup."

She grinned and squeezed his hand.

They got off the train at Salisbury and took the bus to Stonehenge. When she stepped off the bus Trinity felt the heaviness again. It was strong, almost suffocating.

The little gypsy woman was there. Logan nodded to her. She nodded back. To Trinity's surprise they followed the woman down a dirt path to a little cottage.

"Where are we going?" she whispered.

Logan just nodded at the woman they were following.

Trinity followed quietly.

The woman opened the cottage door and motioned for them to come in. Logan and Alaina took a seat, Trinity and Nicholas followed suit. The gypsy sat down in her rocking chair, lit her long curved pipe and began rocking.

Logan introduced them, "Trinity, this is Sabina. Sabina this is Trinity and her twin brother, Nicholas."

"Twins. Interesting," she mused, rocking back and forth.

"Sabina is the Head Guardian," Logan said.

"I know about the Guardians," Trinity said.

Logan looked at her surprised. Samuel must have told her about them.

"Start from the beginning," Trinity said.

Sabina nodded at Logan. He began.

"Near the beginning of time, just after Stonehenge was built, it was used as a portal for demons to flood into the earth's realm. While angels were created with bodies very similar to human form, most demons can only temporarily possess the body of a human. They cannot manifest themselves in human form," Logan began.

"So a flood of demons used the portal to enter the earth's realm and take control of humans as hosts. They possessed thousands of people's bodies. We were overwhelmed, so we ordained a bloodline of humans with quasi-supernatural powers to help us fight the demons. The Guardians. Together we defeated the demons and drove them back to their evil realm. All these burial mounds in the miles surrounding Stonehenge are where we buried the human bodies that the demons possessed after we vanquished them from the hosts. Sometimes the humans survived the vanquishment, but mostly they did not. It depended on how embedded the demon was in the human host."

Everyone was quiet.

"The burial mounds are a reminder of that battle," he continued. "And now, once again, thousands of years later, the demons are trying to use the portal. If they are successful, it will mean another massive slaughter of the human race."

"How am I involved?" Trinity asked.

111

"That will be revealed at the right time," Logan said.

"So the remains buried in Stonehenge, in the center of the circle, who are they?" Trinity asked.

"Those are the original Guardians. The ones that helped defeat the invasion. They were the first. It is a special resting place of honor for them. And the responsibility of being a Guardian has been passed down from generation to generation."

"So the Guardians know which are angels and which are demons?" Nicholas asked.

"Yes."

"So the heaviness and oppression I feel when I am here, what is it?" Trinity asked.

"There's an army mounting in the spiritual realm."

"So you are telling me there is a crap load of demons waiting outside to swarm in at any moment?" Trinity asked.

"Exactly."

"Great," Trinity said, sarcastically.

"So what's your plan to stop them?" she asked.

"There is an army of angels preparing to go to war as well, which is why I have been coming and going," Logan explained. "I will fight. Phoenix, Alaina, and Tristan will also fight."

"How many Guardians are there?" Nicholas asked.

"The number varies but it originally was a specific bloodline. Currently there are ten families who are Guardians of Stonehenge."

"That's not very many," Trinity said, quietly.

The old woman spoke.

"It's been very quiet for many generations. We've not needed a lot of Guardians."

"But there's a war coming. So are we going to need more?" Trinity asked.

"Let's hope not." Logan said.

"So do you know when they are going to try to come through the portal?" she asked.

"We are assuming the night of the competition. There will be thousands of people here, which means thousands of human hosts."

"Yikes!" Trinity said, finally realizing how dire the situation was.

"Will they try to possess me?" she asked.

"I don't think they could. A host has to be slightly receptive, and you aren't at all."

"There will be a lot of young people here for the concert," Trinity said.

"Young people are more receptive to spiritual beings, and the demons are thinking the same thing as well," Logan said.

Trinity started thinking about Roan and everything he had been telling her. Maybe all his talk and chance meetings was to soften her, to make her more receptive to being a host. It scared her. She needed more time to think it all through.

Trinity and Logan walked around Stonehenge circle one more time.

"Did you know that these stones from the inner circle are from Wales, hundreds of miles away?" Logan asked her.

"These huge stones were located 200 miles from here?" she asked, unbelieving.

"Yup."

"Then how did they get here?" she asked, skeptically.

He just smiled at her. She playfully pushed him.

"Seriously! You aren't going to tell me?" she asked.

"Well some things have to remain a mystery, human girl," he said smugly.

She stopped walking. He stopped and stared at her with a silly grin.

"You serious? Like serious, serious?" she asked.

"Yup."

Her mouth gaped.

"You can tell me about thousands of demons that are going to use Stonehenge as a portal to enter our world, but you can't tell me how the stones got here?"

He took a step closer to her, looking down at her.

"Need to know basis for you mortals. As I see it, demons flying through the portal is pertinent information. How the stones got here isn't."

She grabbed his jacket and pulled him towards her. She looked up at his face only inches away.

She grinned, "You are infuriating."

He leaned down and kissed her.

They walked back to the bus.

"So what was Stonehenge created for? Was it created for evil?" she asked.

"Nope."

"So it wasn't created for evil, but the demons somehow used it for evil?"

"Yup."

"You aren't going to tell me who built it, how the rocks got here, or what its original use was for, are you?" she asked.

"Nope."

"Why not?"

He looked at her.

"Ya ya, I get it…need to know, some things need to remain a mystery, blah blah blah," she answered her own question.

Logan swung an arm around her shoulders and they sauntered off to find Nicholas.

Chapter Twenty-Two

Back at the twins' townhouse in London, Mr. and Mrs. Heart had prepared a family dinner. Logan joined them.

"So we are thinking about renting a house in the countryside for the weekend. Are you guys interested in coming with us?" Mr. Heart asked.

"That sounds like a nice change of pace," Trinity said.

"Logan you are welcome to join us for the weekend if you'd like," Mrs. Heart offered.

"Really? That sounds like fun," Logan said, excited at the chance to spend more time with Trinity.

"Nicholas, if your friend Sam will be back by then he is also welcome to come." Their mom offered. "We'll be out there Friday, Saturday and Sunday so he could take the train out anytime."

"I'm not sure when he will be back. He is making his rounds with all his friends right now," Nicholas said.

He looked sideways at his sister and Logan.

"I'm sure he'll be back sometime this summer," Trinity said. "We just left the invitation open," Trinity said.

"Well, he seems like a really nice young man," Mr. Heart told the twins. "I'm really proud of you two. You both have learned to pick your friends well."

"Ya, cuz our friends are ethereal beings," Trinity thought to herself. She grinned at her brother.

He raised one eyebrow at her. He was thinking the exact same thing.

"I'll make sure to let Sam know where we are, so if he stops by he can find us," Nicholas told his parents.

"I wish he would come, it would make the weekend so much fun!" Trinity said, without thinking.

Logan and her brother gave her a look of disapproval.

Face palm.

She just realized how awkward that would be. Logan would not want to share her with Sam.

"We will drive out tomorrow morning," Mrs. Heart said. "How about everyone be ready to leave at ten?"

They all nodded in agreement.

The next morning Trinity was packed and ready to go. Logan showed up with fifteen minutes to spare. They loaded everything into the SUV and Trinity's mom locked the front door.

"Hey guys!" Sam surprised everyone as he walked up with his duffel over his shoulder. "I heard there was a weekend in the country and I didn't want to miss out. Is there still room for me?"

Trinity and Nicholas were shocked that Sam had invited himself. They had actually not said anything to Sam about their weekend trip, thinking it would be too awkward with Logan.

Finally Trinity grinned and Nicholas said, "Of course! Throw your stuff in the back," Nicholas said.

Sam gave Trinity a sly grin.

She blushed.

Logan's expression was hard as stone.

"Oh boy," she thought. "This isn't such a good idea."

Nicholas and Sam climbed into the third row of seats while Logan and Trinity sat in the second row directly behind her parents. Logan pulled Trinity close and kept his arm around her shoulders. He nuzzled his nose in her hair.

"You smell like violets," he mused.

She grinned at him.

From the backseat Nicholas tried to keep Sam's attention, but Sam was watching Trinity.

The ride was entertaining. They all talked about Trinity's upcoming concert at Stonehenge and how exciting that was going to be.

Trinity spent most the ride looking out the window worried about how she would manage with both Sam and Logan. She knew Nicholas would do his best to ease the tension, but she was torn between wanting to spend time with Logan and a growing interest in Sam.

Three hours later they drove through the quaint village where they were spending the weekend.

All of a sudden Trinity sucked in her breath and her body went rigid. Logan noticed immediately.

"What's wrong?" he whispered.

"This town," she said. "It's the one from my dream last year."

"The dreams where Roan chased you and killed you?" he asked.

She nodded.

Last year she had dreams in which Roan tried to kill her. Then at the end of the school year her dreams nearly came true as Roan almost killed her exactly as she had envisioned.

Trinity was uncomfortable. This was weird. She had never been to this village before. She had only seen it in her dreams and now here she was a year later after she had dreamt about it.

They drove through the village and up a dirt road to a beautiful English house. They parked, unloaded the car and explored the house where they would spend the next three days. There were two rooms in the attack, one on each side of stairwell.

Trinity took the attic room looking out the front of the house, and all three boys took the attic room looking out the back. Each of the rooms had vaulted ceilings and gabled windows.

When Trinity was unpacking someone surprised her. He covered her eyes from behind.

"Guess who?" he whispered.

She knew it was Sam. She turned and gave him a big hug.

"Hey, how'd you get in here?" she asked, looking at her closed door.

"There's a secret passage from your room to ours," Sam said, with a gleam in his eye.

"What?" she asked, surprised.

Sam showed her a small door in the back of her closet. The door led to a secret passage, behind the wall and opened into the closet of the boy's room. She made a mental note to shut her closet door just in case the boys unexpectedly decided to use the passage and surprise her while she was changing!

Sam went back to his own room and Trinity went back to hers.

Her door burst open and her brother ran in and jumped on her bed.

"We are gonna go into the village to look around. Coming?" he asked.

She jumped on top of him pushing him off the bed.

"Of course. Let's go!"

She leapt off the bed, rushed into the hallway, grabbed Logan's hand and went down the stairs.

The four friends walked down the gravel driveway toward the village. It was just five minute walk. Logan had his arm around Trinity. Sam and Nicholas walked behind them. Trinity could feel Sam's eyes watching her every move.

Why did she feel this way? Why was she so concerned about what Sam thought? She was just confused. Were they feelings of romance or just friendship and how did Logan fit into it all?

They found a little pub in the main square to have lunch at and grabbed seats outside in the courtyard. Everyone ordered.

"I met Sabina," Trinity told Sam.

Sam looked at Logan. Trinity was not sure what the look meant.

"I told her about the burial mounds and what we expect to happen the night of the concert," Logan explained to Sam. "I also told Trinity and Nicholas about the first time the demons used Stonehenge as a portal and the battle that ensued."

Sam nodded.

There was an awkward silence.

"So Logan, you gonna tell me where you've been while you were gone?" Trinity asked, sweetly.

"Nope."

She pouted playfully.

The food came and everyone ate.

"Trinity, when you dreamed about this village last year, what happened?" Logan asked.

"I was here, in this village, it was the first time I prayed and you showed up to save me," she told him.

121

"So Roan didn't bite you in this one?"

"Nope. But he sure came close. He had his fangs out lunging for my neck. In the next second you were here, your sword guarding my throat from his teeth. Roan left immediately after that."

Logan seemed satisfied with her answer.

Sam looked at Trinity, concerned. She glanced at him briefly. The story bothered him. He was a Protector Angel, and he did not like to hear stories about Trinity in danger.

"You mind telling me more about your dreams?" Sam said.

"Sam, thanks for your concern," Logan said. "But we don't need your help on this."

"It's okay Logan, I don't mind," Trinity said. She looked at her brother and gave him a this-is-an-awkward-weekend look.

"Last year I had several dreams. They all took place in different locations, a field, a castle, this village," she said.

"Have you been here before?" Sam asked.

"No."

"Had you seen this village before?" Sam asked.

"No," answered Trinity. "The first time was in my dream. In each dream I was wearing a formal dress, very gothic-looking. When the dream began I was alone. Then Roan appeared and chased me. Each time, he caught me and he shed his human face and I could see his horrible demon countenance. The first time I had the dream he attacked me and ripped open my stomach with his teeth. In the dreams that followed, I prayed for help and Logan showed up each time, rescuing me from Roan."

Sam glared at Logan. He could not believe Logan did not share this information with him, her Protector. Logan just glared back.

"When you had dreams before, Roan physically attacked you and tore into your flesh with his fangs," said Sam. "And you are having more dreams now? Does he hurt you physically in the new dreams?"

"No. He tries to take me away," she said.

Sam ran his hand through his unruly blonde hair. He looked worried.

"Logan..." he said, warning.

Logan looked at him. Sam stared him down. Logan looked away uncomfortably.

"Oh for goodness sake, tell me what is going on!" Trinity demanded.

"It's nothing," Logan said.

"Stop it Logan," Sam said. "It is something."

Trinity did not know who to believe. She was inclined to believe Sam. He was the one who was the one most concerned about her safety right now.

"Logan, look at me!" she said, sharply. "I get that you have your secrets, but you need to tell me what is going on."

Logan looked at her pleadingly.

"Sam! Tell me!" she said, looking at Sam.

Sam glanced at Logan and cleared his throat.

"You know your dreams come true, right?" Sam said.

She gave him a "duh" look.

"Well, this dream where Roan carries you away is a warning," Sam explained.

She gave him another "duh" look.

"There are certain people who have dreams that are more like premonitions," explained Sam. "When they dream, those dreams come true. You are dreaming the same basic event, but with different surroundings." Sam explained. "It is likely that you have the gift. You should be aware of this gift and use it to your advantage instead of being afraid of it."

"Knowledge is power. Is that what you are saying?" she asked.

"Yes!" Sam looked happy with her.

"So Roan is going to kidnap me. How do I stop it?" she asked.

"For starters, I'm not going to leave your side," Sam said with a defiant look at Logan.

Logan looked away from Sam, he couldn't really argue.

"Either I or Sam will be here at all times," Logan said.

"Kind of seems like I'm hogging an angel when there are thousands of people that are in danger on the night of the concert. We know a demon can't possess me. I'm too strong," she said.

"Right. But that doesn't mean he won't try to take you away or worse, kill you. You are important in all this," Sam said.

"Yes, you care to explain how I am important in all this?" she said, smartly.

Sam grinned. "Nope."

She growled.

He pulled his head back. "Did you just growl at me?" he asked with an amused grin.

"Yup." she said, smugly, and leaned back in her chair folding her arms over her chest.

"I think maybe Trinity contracted rabies when Roan bit her," Sam teased.

"I haven't noticed any foaming of the mouth, but I'll keep my eyes out for it," Logan said.

Trinity threw a French fry at Sam.

"Oh hush up you two," she said, laughing.

"You see that?" Sam jested. "Aggressive behavior. You sure she hasn't been foaming at the mouth?"

Trinity threw another French fry.

"Roar" she said sarcastically.

They all laughed.

Chapter Twenty-Three

On the way back to the house the four ran into a group of teens. There was going to be a big game of capture the flag tonight, after dark, in the village. Roman, a lanky and handsome rogue seemed to be the organizer.

"You guys interested?" Roman asked.

"Ya!" Trinity exclaimed, quickly.

"Well, we probably should talk it over first," Logan said, looking at Trinity.

"What's there to talk over? Either you're in or you're out," Roman said.

"We are in," Trinity replied.

"We are meeting back here at nine in the evening to go over the rules and boundaries. We'll split up teams then. See you guys later," Roman said.

Trinity was giddy. It was going to be so much fun to have a full scale capture the flag game throughout the entire village.

When they were out of ear shot of the other teens, Logan gently took her arm.

"What?" she said, startled

"The village. Night time. Roan. Ring any bells Trinity?" he asked.

"Ya I know. Sounds a lot like my dream from last year. But I can't live my entire life not doing anything because I'm afraid the dreams will come true," she said.

Logan sighed.

"Besides, you or Sam will be on my team and can keep an eye on me."

Sam smiled.

"And none of that stealth mode, Mr. Sammy," she teased. "You have to play fair with these mortals."

Sam smiled and disappeared right in front of her. "Like this?" he asked, invisible.

Trinity felt an invisible hand tousle her hair.

"No, none of that," Trinity laughed, shaking her hair.

That afternoon they sat around and played board games. It was nice to have a break from the madness.

When eight o'clock rolled around everyone dressed in dark clothes. Trinity wore black pants, a black, fitted hoodie and a black beanie pulled down over her braided hair. In the dark she would be nearly invisible.

They met the other teens in the village square. The rules were explained. The village was divided in two by the main road running down the middle. You could not leave the village. The goal was to capture the other team's flag and make it back to your own side without getting caught. If you were caught on the opposing team's side, you went to jail. The only way out of jail was for one of your own team members to risk running to the jail and tagging you out and both of you had to make it back to your territory safely.

Roman put Trinity and Nicholas on his team and Sam and Logan on the other team. Trinity looked nervous. The plan was for at least one of the angels to be on her team. Sam quickly spoke up.

"Hey I'm gonna trade places with Nicholas."

Roman just waved his hand that it was fine. Logan gave Sam an angry glare.

The flags were assigned to their spots and each team went off to make their plans. Roman told Trinity to stick close to him. She began to get the feeling he kind of liked her. Sam's was near Trinity. He planned on staying close to her.

The clock started and everyone scattered. Trinity and Roman were going to try to capture the other team's flag. Sam tagged along at a distance, not revealing himself to Roman.

"I haven't seen you around here," Roman whispered.

"We are just here visiting for the weekend," she explained, quietly.

"Too bad," he said.

"Too bad?" she asked.

"Ya, it woulda been nice to have you around," Roman teased.

"Duck!" Roman whispered, fiercely, grabbing Trinity and pulling her down behind a car.

They had not entered enemy territory yet, but they saw one of the other team's players sneaking along the wall.

Roman motioned that he and Trinity should split up, one wait for the enemy to come to their corner and the other to circle around the house to block him in. Trinity nodded. She headed around the house, sneaking slowly and deliberately. Soon the enemy was between her and Roman. They ran at the enemy together and caught the girl. The two of them took her to the jail.

They went back to their position looking for their opportunity to sneak into the enemy territory. To cross the dividing line between the territories, they would be exposed on the well-lit road for a second. They waited and watched for any movement, anyone on the other side waiting for them.

It seemed like hours, but it was only ten minutes while they waited. They were hunched down in a dark shadow in the crevice of a building.

"Where you from?" Roman asked.

"U.S." she said. "But I go to school at Shadowland."

"Nice," he said. "We should cross the line now."

They looked around once more and together crossed the line and hid in the shadows of a building. They waited another five minutes before moving. Trinity knew Sam was close by. She could feel him. She was pretty sure he had crossed the line a block away.

Roman and Trinity carefully crept another block. They heard feet running towards them. Roman grabbed Trinity and threw her into the crevice between two of the buildings and covered her mouth.

There was barely enough room for them. She could feel his chest rising and falling and heart beating wildly due to adrenaline. She stayed there, awkwardly, yet silent. One of the enemy team ran right by them and continued up the street.

Roman peeked out. He moved his hand from her mouth.

"Sorry. Just didn't want you to give away our hiding spot."

"Yes because I want to sit in their jail," she said, smartly.

They maneuvered out of their tight hiding spot. Roman took her hand and led the way. She was not sure what to make of it, but decided to just let him hold her hand since he was guiding her between buildings in the pitch dark.

He squeezed her hand and they ducked behind a sidewalk sign when they saw another one of the enemy slinking along the other side of the street. They waited quietly until the enemy was gone.

"It's going to be tricky getting to the flag without being seen and I'm sure there is at least one person guarding it," Roman said.

"The closest I think we could get undetected is to the little café with the tables and chairs in the square," she said.

Roman agreed.

"But I am thinking we should throw a decoy out there to get caught and bring out the enemy that is guarding the flag," he suggested.

She looked at him.

"You suggesting I run out as a decoy?" she asked, sourly.

Roman grinned handsomely.

"Of course not sweets."

"Then who?" she asked, with a sassy tone.

"Your little friend that is following us around," he whispered, matter-of-factly, close to her face.

Trinity knew Sam was near, but she had not seen him. How could Roman have possibly seen him?

"Where is Sam?" she asked, looking around.

"I don't know where he is right now but I saw him cross the road behind us," Roman said.

"Then how are we to find him?" she asked Roman.

"I don't know, I was kind of hoping he would catch up with us," Roman said, looking around the square.

Trinity knew how to get him to come to her, but she was not sure she wanted to use it for a game. It was reserved for times when she was in trouble. She decided against it. She would just have to wait for him.

They waited in the dark.

Silence.

"You have a boyfriend?" Roman asked, breaking the silence.

And there it is, thought Trinity.

"Kinda," she said, unsure how to answer that question considering her boyfriend was an angel.

"Kinda?" he asked, amused.

"Ya well, it's complicated," she said, dryly.

"No need to get bent out of shape, sweets," Roman said.

"I'm not," she said, honestly.

"Wanna try something uncomplicated?" he asked, with a grin.

She did not know if he was teasing or serious.

"Some days," she answered.

Roman chuckled.

She shrugged.

Movement caught Trinity's eye. There was someone across the square waiting in the shadows. She did not know if it was one of their teammates or one of the enemies. She strained to see if she recognized anything. Nothing.

Trinity did not want her voice to carry now that she knew there was another person in the vicinity. She grabbed Romans face with her hand and turned it to look at the shadow across the square. He turned his head back to her and nodded. They sat in silence.

"Come on Sam, where are you?" she thought.

She looked around the square for any other movement. They now knew where one of the players was hiding. There was a good chance there was another one.

Trinity nearly startled when she saw a figure slinking along the brick wall they leaned against. She recognized the figure as Sam. She was relieved.

"We were wondering when you were gonna show up," Roman said.

"You guys were sitting here for so long I thought maybe something was up," Sam said.

"We've spotted one of the enemies. But we think there is another one," she said.

"So I'm thinking maybe we send in a decoy. Cause a distraction and then send in two more to snag the flag and we all make a break for it and meet back at the truck two blocks away," Sam suggested.

"Exactly," Roman agreed.

"I'm guessing I'm the distraction?" Sam asked, wryly.

"Exactly!" they both replied in unison.

Sam chuckled.

The three of them slinked up to the café where they could still stay in cover. Then Sam darted out in the open running towards the flag. Suddenly, the figure that had been hiding in the shadows across the plaza jumped out and chased after him. Roman and Trinity waited to see if a second person came out, but no one did.

Roman and Trinity ran towards the flag, while Sam ran zig-zags around the square keeping the enemy on his tail. A second enemy jumped out right near Trinity, she yelped and ran towards the flag. Roman cut the enemy off and they chased him instead. Trinity grabbed the flag and ran out of the plaza. She held onto the flag tightly and did not stop running.

It was not till she was several blocks away that she darted into a dark alley and caught her breath. She tied the bandana flag around her wrist so she did not have to carry it anymore. She could not remember how to get to the truck; she had run too far out of the way. She was going to have to sneak back to her side of the village without getting caught on her own. She hoped Sam did not freak out.

She poked her head out from the alley. The coast seemed clear. She slithered across the street and ducked behind a car. She waited to see if anything moved around her. Her heart beat heavily and she could hear her pulse in her ears. She moved again, one block over and one block up towards what she thought was the middle road that divided the village. She slipped into the crevice of a building and waited again. The key, was to slowly and patiently make her way back.

She stood in the shadow and waited. Across the street was another crevice, she tried to see any movement in the darkness. Suddenly she saw a small red light and wisp of smoke. She instinctively backed up a step, deeper into the crevice.

The red light and smoke appeared again. Trinity knew it was a cigarette. Someone was in the shadow smoking. She did not know if they were a part of the game or if they were just out for an evening smoke. Now she could not move until they did. So she waited.

A few minutes later a dark figure slinked out of the crevice across the road and headed down the street. Trinity thought his saunter was vaguely familiar but she did not think it was someone in the game. She waited another few minutes before she peeked out. She looked down the road and turned to look the other way when someone pushed her back into the shadowy crevice and held her against the wall.

Roan!

"Heya Pet," he crooned.

"Roan," she whispered, her breath sucking in sharply.

"Surprised to see me?" he asked, confused. "Come now doll, you and I both know this village has special meaning for us."

She groaned.

"Oh but don't worry Pet, I'm not gonna bite you tonight," he said, with a wicked grin.

She was relieved. This was just going to be another attempt to bring her to the dark side.

"Listen Roan, I'm in the middle of a game. I've got the flag around my wrist and Sam and Logan are both here. You really wanna do this right now?" she asked.

He chuckled and grabbed her wrist pinning it to the side of her head. He glanced at the red flag tied around her arm.

"So you are playing a game," he said, glancing out to the street nervously and releasing her wrist.

"Nervous?" she asked him, growing confident.

He chuckled again.

"It would be so much more fun to play games with me, you know," he said, his voice dripping with sensuality.

"Now's not the time," she said, sternly. "And I'm guessing you have a few seconds before Sam shows up ready to kick your sorry butt, so I'd run along if I were you."

He smiled.

"Okay Pet, have it your way this time."

He leaned in and smelled her. His lips quivered.

"Delicious," he whispered and left.

Trinity shuddered.

She glanced down the street and ran the other way. She was not going to stay around there very long and she needed to get to the other side of the village before they sent a search party out for her.

She bobbed and weaved around the cottages. She looked around and moved slowly through the streets trying to remember which way she was supposed to go.

Finally, she recognized one of the streets and knew she was close. One block away. She breathed deeply and bolted for the main road. She was two blocks away but it was a straight shot. She just had to get there without getting caught.

Her feet slapped against the pavement. If anyone was within the vicinity they would hear her and come running. Sure enough one block from the line someone fell in behind her, chasing her.

"She's got the flag! Get her!" she heard one boy yell.

She ran faster. There were two sets of feet chasing her now. Fifty feet to the line. Forty feet. Thirty. The boys drew closer to her. Her lungs burned. Twenty feet...ten feet. She leapt across the road just as the boys missed grabbing her.

She hit the ground, rolled over on her back and breathed deeply. She had just won the game for her team.

"Game over!" some of the kids yelled out.

Everyone started to come out of their hiding spots and gathered again in the main square. "You had me nervous. Glad you're okay," Sam whispered.

"I'm fine," she said, smiling.

Roman ran over to her.

"I knew you could do it, sweets," he said, grinning.

"What took you so long to get to our side?" he asked.

"I just wanted to be careful," Trinity said.

"Mmmm. Smart and sweet," Roman crooned. She laughed and backed away. He was getting a little too friendly.

Everyone decided that since that game took almost two hours they would try to play again the following night instead of fitting in another game on the same night.

Roman gave Trinity a little wave as they parted ways. Logan noticed and swung his arm around Trinity's shoulders protectively as they walked back to the house.

"We didn't even see you guys the entire game," Nicholas said.

"Were you on offense or defense?" Trinity asked. They told her they were both on offense.

"Well so were we, so we wouldn't run into one another most likely," she said.

Trinity hoped they would get to play again the following night. She had so much fun.

She decided to keep the Roan incident to herself. He had not harmed her. Plus, if she told the boys they would never let her play again tomorrow night.

When she got back she climbed into bed. She was tired and satisfied with her performance this evening. It was nice to have a semi-normal evening once in a while. She said a little prayer of thanks and quickly she drifted off to sleep with a smile on her face.

Chapter Twenty-Four

In the morning everyone gathered in the large country kitchen for pancakes and bacon. Trinity scarfed down her food. All the running last night made her hungry.

"How was the game last night?" her mom asked.

"Trinity won it for their team," her brother said, proudly.

"Nice," her mom said, smiling.

"Well, I had the help of Sam and Roman. I couldn't have done it without them," Trinity offered.

Sam gave grinned at her across the table.

"We offered them up as bait," she added, smugly.

Her mom laughed.

"Did they get caught?" she asked.

"No ma'am," Sam said.

"Well then, sounds like it worked out for your team," her dad said.

"Yes sir," Sam said, grinning at Trinity.

Logan sat quietly. Trinity knew he had wanted to be on her team. But honestly she felt like Sam would protect her better against Roan, only because Roan seemed to be really scared of him. She was not sure if it was wrong of her to feel that way. She convinced herself it was because Roan feared Sam more than he feared Logan.

After breakfast everyone got ready and decided to visit one of the local castles. It was only thirty minutes away. They all road in the car together.

When they pulled up, Trinity went rigid. The castle was familiar. It was not in the same shape as it had been in her dream from last year, but it was definitely the same one.

Logan looked at her, concerned.

"The same castle?" he asked.

She nodded.

Nicholas took Trinity aside before they went in.

"You okay?" he asked.

"Same castle as in my dream from last year," she told him.

"Same village, same castle, I don't like this sis."

She shrugged.

"You worried?" he asked.

"Not really."

"Cuz of them?" Nick asked, nodding towards the two angels waiting for them.

"Not really."

"Then what?"

"Not sure."

"Huh," her twin mused, curious.

"Ya."

"If you're cool, I'm cool," he said.

"I'm cool."

"Ok. I'm cool."

And the two of them went back to her parents and the angels.

"Okay, let's do this thing," Nicholas said.

Everyone went inside.

Trinity stayed close to Logan and Sam. She was amazed at how she could have dreamed the exact same castle even though she had never been here before. If it was the same, there was a dungeon and she did not want to go down there. That was where she had been attacked in her dream.

Trinity's parents were nearby the entire time, as were Sam and Logan. Trinity was sure Roan would not try to make another appearance with so many people protecting her. He always approached her when she was alone.

Her parents wanted to see the dungeon. Trinity hesitated, but went with them. Logan kept his arm around her the entire time. She saw the cell where she was attacked in her dreams. How could she have seen all this?

After exploring the castle they went back to the village to have lunch.

"How'd you like the Oxford campus?" her dad asked her.

"I like it," Trinity said, excitedly.

So you're looking for Oxford to notice you on the Lacrosse field this season," her dad said.

"Exactly," she said.

"What about you Nicholas? Where are you looking to go to college?" their mom asked.

"Same," he said.

Nicholas had already been offered two scholarships for swimming: one to Oxford, the other to an Ivy League college in the states.

"So the two of you are going to attend the same college?" Mom asked.

"Sounds like it," Trinity said.

"And here in England as well? Seems like this country has made an impression on you two," her dad said.

"I like London," Trinity said.

"Have you thought about where you are going to go for your senior trip?" Mom asked.

The twin's parents had offered to pay for an international trip after their senior year of high school. They would be eighteen after all, and as long as they stuck together their parents thought it was a great idea.

The twins looked at each other and shrugged. They had not even talked about it. They had so much on their plate with all these "ethereal issues" that their vacation had been put on the back burner.

"We haven't even talked about it," Nicholas said.

"We'll figure it out this year," Trinity said.

"When do we need to know?" Nicholas asked.

Their parents shrugged.

"You don't need to make any decisions until the end of your senior year if you don't want to. Travel plans can be made anytime," Mom said.

Trinity looked at Nicholas. He smiled back at her. He knew what she was thinking. She would want to find out if Logan could come with them. The problem was she was conflicted because she also wanted Sam to come, and that would be weird.

Everyone drove back to the house. Trinity decided to take a nap and Nicholas and Logan took a walk into town. Sam grabbed a book and sat on the front porch swing, occupying himself. He would have gone with the boys but they agreed someone should stay near Trinity.

Trinity woke up from her nap and ventured out to the porch to sit with Sam.

"Hey pal Sammy," she said.

"Hey pal Trinity," he teased back.

The swing moved gracefully back and forth. Trinity pulled her legs up and crossed them on the swing. Sam leaned over and poked her cheek.

"How you been?" he asked.

She looked at him. She knew he meant deep down how was she coping with everything she was experiencing and everything she knew was to come. Three simple words was such a deep question.

"I'm okay," she said, calmly.

"Please elaborate," he said quietly.

"I'm at peace," she said, smiling at him assuredly.

"Really?" he asked, bewildered.

"Really," she said.

"Pal Trinity, you amaze me."

"Pal Sammy, you amaze me."

They smiled.

Chapter Twenty-Five

All the teens met back in the village square. Darkness had fallen. Everyone was dressed in black, ready for battle. Roman assigned the same teams as last night. He told Trinity they were going to stick together again. She was not unhappy with that decision. Roman knew the village and he knew how to play this game.

The game began and Roman pulled Trinity off to the edge of the village. They were going to go on the offense again, but they would try a different tactic tonight. On the outskirts of the village they could see the fields around them and hear the stream that ran alongside the village. They tucked into a side street. Roman led her through the maze. They crept low and slinked along walls in the shadows avoiding all the street lamps.

"You think Sam's nearby again?" he asked Trinity.

"Yup."

"How do you know?" he asked.

"He's good at this stealth stuff," she said.

He smiled.

They saw movement out of the corner of their eyes. They were still on their side of the village so they were the predators. Roman pulled her into a shadow. They stayed quiet while they waited and watched for movement.

Sure enough, someone sneaked across the line and almost crawled down the other side of the street.

"It's the enemy," Roman whispered in her ear.

She nodded.

"You wanna catch them or keep going?" he asked.

"Let's go get 'em," she said, eagerly.

"Ah sweets, that's what I like about you," he said, grinning.

"If you come up behind him and I circle back around the corner we can trap him," Trinity said.

"Sounds good."

She pushed her way out of the hiding place and crept back around the cottage. Roman followed the enemy from behind, cutting off his path back towards his own side of the village.

Trinity popped up around the cottage just as Logan came face to face with her. She grabbed him.

"You're caught," she said, grinning from ear to ear. Although she felt as though maybe he meant to get caught.

Roman came up behind them and they took Logan to their jail. They knew they had to journey back to their previous hiding place, but catching Logan was a good move on their part.

"See ya later babe," Logan said as she walked away.

"Later babe," she teased.

Trinity and Roman ran off in another direction. They made their way back to the edge of the village. They sat in the shadows waiting and watching to see if anyone moved. Before they crossed over into the enemy territory they needed to make sure no one was watching.

Trinity looked back across the street. She saw a red light and a wisp of smoke as she had seen the other night.

Roan! She knew it was him. He was watching her. She glared in his direction. She knew he was grinning at her.

"Ready?" Roman asked.

"Ya."

"Let's go," he said, and pulled her along behind him. They crossed the enemy line and ducked into the shadows to wait and watch before they moved again. Five minutes passed and they saw nothing. They moved forward one block.

"Stay right here," he instructed her. "I'm going to peek around the corner and come back. They usually set up a guard on that corner up there."

She nodded and tucked in the side of a building. She waited while Roman ran off. She looked around. She kept an eye out to make sure they did not get flanked. She saw Roan leaning against the wall with his cigarette. He gave her a sly grin. She rolled her eyes. He tossed the cigarette and sauntered towards her.

"Seriously?" she said, exasperated.

"Hey Pet," he said, brushing her up against the wall.

"Roman is going to be back any second. How in the world would I explain you?" she said, trying to appeal to his common sense, even though she knew he had none.

Roan just chuckled. He held her chin with his fingers and pulled her face up towards his.

"You like the danger of it all," he cooed.

She gave him a sour look.

"Oh come now, Pet, it's exciting that we might get caught," he said, grinning.

"No. More like stressful," she said.

He tried to pull her lips to his, but she pulled away enough to avoid a kiss.

"Ah baby, don't be coy." He played hurt.

"Get lost, Roan," she warned, looking out to the street.

"You gonna tell me Sam and Logan are close?"

"Well they are," she assured him.

"Kinda dangerous for me too, huh?"

She tried to shove him away. But he was stronger than she was. She heard footsteps and peered around the corner hoping to see Sam. It was Roman. When she looked back to warn Roan he was gone. She breathed a sigh of relief.

Roman ran around the corner.

"We gotta move, there are two people headed our way."

They ran down the street and around the corner. But it was too late.

"Run!" Roman yelled.

They broke into a sprint. Roman made sure she was with him every step of the way. Trinity was sure they were going to be caught. They were deep in the enemy territory right now and they needed to hide instead of trying to get back to their side of the village. Trinity was getting tired and just as they rounded the corner, a little old lady with a kerchief and apron stood in her doorway and waved them inside.

Roman ran into the house, pulling Trinity with him. The little old lady shut the door behind them. Trinity doubled over with exhaustion.

"Thank you," she said between gasps. "Is this allowed?"

He could not talk so he just nodded. The little old woman gestured to the small parlor area and the two of them collapsed on the couch. The little old lady brought two cups of tea. Trinity sat up properly and accepted the tea, as did Roman.

"Thank you again ma'am," Trinity said, politely.

"Just call me Grandma Clay," she said, sweetly.

"Thank you, Grandma Clay," she said, again.

"Thanks, grandma," Roman said.

"Wait, is she your grandma?" Trinity asked.

Roman grinned.

"How long should we stay here?" she asked.

"Well we aren't leaving without some mint ice cream," Roman said.

Grandma Clay hurried off into the kitchen.

"She really your Grandma?" Trinity asked.

He nodded.

"Ya, she always helps me out when she can," he admitted.

"Sneaky. Sneaky. Mr. Roman."

He grinned.

Grandma Clay came out of the kitchen with two pretty little bowls of mint ice cream. The two fugitives ate it quickly.

"Now go get 'em kids," Grandma Clay said, a gleam in her eye.

"Yes ma'am," Roman said.

The two of them snuck out the back door and sat in the shadows for a few minutes watching their surroundings. No movement. They crept forward another block and sat in the shadows. They cut through the backyard of a cottage and crept around the garden. They saw movement and they backed into the row of corn lined against a fence. They sat squatting, waiting and watching. A figure walked past the front of the house. They exited out of the garden going the opposite way that the enemy went.

They were just two blocks away from the flag. They had heard two people get caught. So they knew their team was down at least two players. More could have been caught while they were in Grandma Clay's house. Trinity wondered if Sam had been caught. She highly doubted it. But he might have lost their trail when they rushed inside Grandmas' house.

150

They sat outside the village square where the enemy flag resided. Once again, they needed a third person. They crept a little closer and went to squeeze into a little gap between two of the buildings. Roman realized there was someone else in the gap and startled. Trinity almost yelped.

"Wait!" Roman whispered. "It's one of ours."

The player in the gap was someone from their side, an ally, just what they needed. The three of them made a plan. They were going to try the same stunt they had the night before. The third kid ran out into the open as bait. Sure enough, someone came running after him.

Then Roman and Trinity ran out and another person chased them. Then a third person appeared and chased Trinity. No one could reach the flag. They all ran in separate directions to try to save themselves with the enemy right behind.

Trinity ran hard and fast. She leaped over a small fence into someone's backyard and rolled under the small deck before her attacker could round the corner. He kept running by. She stayed in hiding, waiting. She waited for what seemed like an hour and slowly crept out. She moved down the street and hid about two blocks from where the flag was.

She needed to formulate a plan. How was she going to do this by herself? Did Sam and Roman get caught? She could circle around to view the jail and see if they were there. It might be better if she sprung one of them from jail and then she would have a partner in crime.

She poked out of her hiding spot and came face to face with Roan. She groaned.

"Ah shucks Pet, I thought this might be a better time, since you're all alone," he said.

"No time is good," she muttered under her breath.

He pushed himself in between the buildings with her.

"Come on Roan. I'm not going to come to the dark side," she said. "You said you weren't going to devour me, so this really is an exercise in futility isn't it?"

"Maybe. But it's so much fun," he crooned in her ear.

This was getting ridiculous. He simply wanted to feed off of these little moments together. Yes, the danger was exciting in a scary way, but she also knew that Roan, underneath that witty smile and charming looks was an evil, ugly, sinister demon that had once tried to kill her.

She snapped back to reality quickly remembering that cold winter night where she almost bleed out. She shoved Roan away. She maneuvered her way out of the side street and figured she might as well give herself up to the enemy team. To get away from Roan she was going to have to walk out into the open.

Roan grabbed her from behind. "Wait Pet, don't give yourself up. I'll leave."

He brushed past her, letting his hand slide over her waist. He turned towards her one last time and brushed her cheek with his hand.

"You still don't feel anything?" he asked, befuddled.

"Nope."

"I don't know how, but you've bewitched me, Pet."

She grimaced. He disappeared.

She stayed in her hiding spot figuring out her next move. She decided to check out the jail and see if she could spring Roman. She made her way over to the jail. She saw Roman and one other player there. She could only spring one person from the jail and they would have to make it back over to their own side without getting caught.

"Psst," she whispered at Roman from her hiding spot. He looked over towards the shadows. She poked her head out and he saw her. She gave him a nod and he knew she was going to spring him from his imprisonment.

She looked both ways, knew where the enemy was and made a run for the jail. She successfully tagged Roman out and they ran for their side of the village. They had to make it all the way without getting caught or they would go back to jail.

They were running as fast as they could for their own side. They could hear the sound of two people running after them. Trinity did not want to look back and see who it was, she just knew she had to run faster.

"Run Trinity. Don't look back," Roman said as he ran in front of her. She obeyed.

The footsteps got closer. There was no time to hide or take a turn, they had to run straight down the street towards the center road dividing the two territories. Roman was taller and could run faster. He was out fifteen feet in front of her and the steps behind her drew close. She knew she was not going to make it.

Slam! Arms grabbed her from behind, the motion swung her around. She doubled over in pain, her lungs burned. Roman had made it over the line. He was safe. She was captured.

The price for his freedom was hers. He turned back and saw her being dragged to the enemy jail.

Trinity sat quietly in prison, surveying her surroundings. It was dark and she had a hard time seeing. She knew Roman was now free, but she did not think he would risk coming to rescue her. Sam was also out there, but he may not even know that she had been caught. It was more likely that Sam and Roman would team up, snatch the flag and the game would be over soon.

She stood waiting and watching. There was nobody else in the jail. Apparently while she was springing Roman, someone else freed the other person that had been in jail. She was alone. She knew there was a guard hidden somewhere in the shadows. The night was silent. No sounds of kids running. No sounds of dogs barking. It was eerie.

She heard footsteps pattering against the cobblestone street. Someone was coming. They were being too loud to be one of her team mates. She saw a figure approach at a run. It was her brother. He stopped outside the jail and laughed.

"Got caught, eh sis."

She stared at him.

"Well glad you're in there. You seem to be really good at this game."

"Gee thanks."

He chuckled and ran off.

She sighed. She did not like being stuck here. She hoped Roman would come back for her, but she knew better.

"Psst." The noise came from the shadows behind her.

She turned around, careful not to draw any attention to herself. Sam stood in the shadows. He tagged her out and they slipped away into the darkness quietly.

"You came to get me," she said, surprised.

"Of course."

"Why? You could have just retrieved the flag and ended the game."

He grinned.

"It's much more fun running around in the dark with you," he said, guiding her down the street.

"You know where Roman is?" she asked.

He shook his head.

"Let's get back to our side safely and then make a run for the flag," Trinity said.

Sam and Trinity snuck around corners in the shadows of the village. They cut through a couple backyards to avoid the streets where there was no place to hide. They heard someone coming their way and they dashed behind a little cottage and hid behind the garden shed.

Sam still held her hand. She looked down at it in the dark. He caught her looking and looked down as well. They looked at each other and if it had not been dark she was sure he could see her blush. He did not let go. The hand holding was not for romance, but necessity in the game. It allowed you to communicate in the dark without speaking. A squeeze, a tug, even dragging your partner along so you didn't get separated. At least that she told herself. She was pretty sure the boys didn't hold hands.

He turned his attention back to the street, scoping out their escape plan.

They ventured a couple more blocks and soon had safely crossed to their side of the village. They were now the hunters, not the hunted.

Trinity breathed a sigh of relief. She had been the hunted for so long, not just in this game, but in life. Right now Sam, her Protector Angel, was with her and she was safe.

"Let's go get the flag," Trinity said.

They turned and ran towards the edge of the village. They would cross the line into enemy territory and work their way towards the center of the village. Once they crossed the line, they stayed in the shadows. They were close to the village center where the enemy flag was. The two of them ran out into the open and Trinity was able to snatch the flag and run. Sam tried to out distract the attacker. But it was Nicholas and he was determined to catch her.

She ran as hard as she could. She knew there was a little park up ahead and she could jump into the bushes and hide if she got there fast enough. Her brother was fast on her tail. There would be no time. She would have to run all the way to her side of the village without getting caught. She entered the park and saw the stone wall in front of her, it was about thigh high and she jumped over it.

Trinity screamed.

On the other side of the wall, was the river that ran through the village. She fell ten feet down into the rushing water. Her brother leaned over the edge and saw his sister in the dark, cold water.

"HELP!" HELP!" she screamed.

Trinity tread water the best she could. The current was pulling her downstream. She tried to fight the current but knew sooner or later she would not be able to. Her brother yelled for help. A few more kids showed up. Her limbs started to go numb. She thought she was going to die.

Trinity prayed a short prayer. She knew Sam and Logan would both hear it. They would save her. The rock wall was about ten feet down to the river and no one could reach her. They looked around for something to pull her up with.

Her body went numb.

"Please help," she half prayed, half cried.

She gave up and let the current started to drag her down the river. Someone dove into the water and grabbed her. They were swept down river together.

"Don't worry, I've got you," Sam's voice assured.

Her lips quivered and her teeth chattered.

"Just hold onto me, I will warm you. I will keep us afloat," he told her.

She turned and wrapped her arms around him and her legs around his waist. Miraculously she began to warm. She still shivered, but she was not frozen any longer, only cold. She could feel her limbs again.

The two of them moved swiftly down the river channel. Above, Trinity saw kids running along the wall, watching them. They moved into a tunnel where the river ran underground. It was pitch black. Trinity could not see anything. She could only feel Sam holding her tightly and his cheek against hers.

"You're safe, Trinity. You will be okay. I will save you," he whispered in her ear, reassuringly. She clung to him. She knew she was safe. She knew she would live. She knew Sam would save her.

They came out of the underwater tunnel and they heard the kids above yelling at them.

"You guys okay?"

"Yes!" Sam yelled. "Meet us at the village edge."

At the end of the village the wall ended and gave way to a green, grassy river bank where Sam could pull them out.

"You warm enough?" he asked.

"I don't know. I'm cold. But I can feel my fingers and toes," she said through chattering teeth.

He squeezed her tightly and she felt a rush of warmth run through her. The edge of the village was near. Somehow Sam propelled them to the side of the river. When they came to the grassy bank, everyone was there. Sam put out his hand and Logan grabbed it, pulling them out of the water. Her brother covered her with a blanket and gave one to Sam as well.

She was shivering. Her brother gave her a big hug. No words were needed. When he was done Logan embraced her, relieved. She gave him a weak smile.

"Let's go home," he said.

158

"Wait!" she said. "Whose side of the village are we on?"

Roman looked at her and grinned.

"We are on our side, safe territory."

She pulled out the flag from her pocket and showed everyone.

"I guess we win," she said smugly through her chattering teeth.

Roman broke out laughing.

"Well Sweets, aren't you quite the player!"

He looked pleased.

Everyone laughed and congratulated her. Logan led her back to the house. Sam and Nicholas walked behind. Logan would not let go of her. They quietly went up to their rooms.

Logan gave Trinity one last hug and went to bed. Nicholas squeezed her tightly. Sam stared at her. She threw her arms around him and held him tightly.

"Thank you," she whispered.

"Nothing bad is ever going to happen to you," he whispered back.

"I believe you," she said.

He gave her another squeeze and let her go. She smiled at him and went into the bathroom to shower. Afterwards, she opened the bathroom door and Sam was waiting outside the door for his turn. His shirt was off and he had a towel in hand. She moved out of the way and watched him go into the bathroom.

He had tattoos. Warrior angels, like Logan, had tattoos as well. Sam's were different. His were a series of symbols. They looked like letters from a strange alphabet, written in a column down the left side of his spine.

Trinity curled up in bed, and tried to go to sleep. She lay awake. All she could think about was her near-death experience. After an hour staring at the ceiling she grabbed a blanket, went downstairs and out to the porch swing. She cuddled up with her warm blanket and swung back and forth gently while she watched the bats and owls fly around.

The screen door opened and Sam came out carrying two mugs. He handed one to her. It was filled with hot chocolate with tiny marshmallows on top.

"This is kinda is becoming our spot," he mused.

She smiled. She liked the idea. She sipped her hot chocolate. They swung in silence. After a while Sam spoke.

"You feel okay, since the dunk in the river?"

"Ya," she smiled at him.

"You can feel all your fingers and toes?"

"Yup."

"I'm glad you said a little prayer."

"Me too," she whispered. "I knew you'd come."

Sam smiled to himself. He had a strong urge to protect her, more than he ever had for any of the humans he protected in the past. He could not understand it. He could not explain it. It just was.

She sipped her chocolate again. A couple bats flew in across the porch. An owl hooted in the dark and a coyote howled. No words were needed. They just sat and enjoyed the night. Trinity started to get sleepy. She nodded off.

Chapter Twenty-Six

Morning came and Trinity woke up in her bed. She was confused. The last thing she remembered was sitting on the swing outside with Sam and a mug of hot chocolate. Yet, she woke up snuggled in her bed.

She threw off the covers. She smelled bacon and coffee. She ran downstairs. Her dad handed her a mug of coffee and gestured to the flavored creamer.

"Thanks," she said, softly. "I need it."

"Well it's almost noon, Sleepyhead," he teased.

"Am I the only one still asleep?" she asked.

He nodded at the three boys clamoring down the stairs in their pajamas. She and her dad chuckled.

"Guess I was the early riser," she muttered to him under her breath.

"Just in time boys," said Trinity's dad. "I knew the smell of fried pig would wake you."

The boys poured themselves coffee and sat on the barstools watching Mr. Heart cook the bacon and eggs.

Trinity gave Sam a sideways glance. She wanted to ask him how she ended up in her bed last night, but she did not want to ask him in front of everyone.

They all gathered around the kitchen table for breakfast, as Trinity's mom walked in the back door. She had been out for a morning run.

"Perfect timing," said Mr. Heart.

"Well, only if you want a sweaty mom at the table," said Mrs. Heart.

"It's okay. You can sit at the end with the boys," Mr. Heart joked.

After breakfast, Trinity lingered while Logan and Nicholas went upstairs. She cornered Sam.

"How'd I get in my bed last night?" she asked him. "All I remember was sitting in the swing…and then nothing."

"I carried you back to bed," he said, nonchalantly.

"You carried me up the stairs?" she asked, bewildered.

He shrugged.

She pushed him playfully.

"Shrug, shrug, shrug. That all you can do?" she teased.

He shrugged again and grinned.

163

Trinity playfully smacked him. He turned to shield himself and ran into the family room.

"You are not getting away so easily," she said, reaching to muss his curly hair.

He stepped aside defensively, dodging her advance. Her momentum sent her crashing onto the couch.

He pretended he was about to dive on top of her but stopped as she squealed. They both laughed and he plopped down on the couch next to her. Their shoulders were touching.

Trinity flushed. She jumped up, and grabbed his hand, pulling him off the couch.

"Time to get ready, Mr. Couch Potato," she teased.

They ran upstairs to get ready to pack for the trip home.

Trinity used the car ride home to nap. It had been a good weekend, but everyone was tired. When they got back to their townhome in London, everyone plopped wearily on the nearest couch or chair.

"I think we should watch movies and get take-out," Nicholas suggested.

"Well, you kids got a nap on the ride home, so I'm going to get mine now," Mr. Heart announced.

"Me too," said Mrs. Heart. "Money's on the counter if you want take-out."

They thanked Mrs. Heart, but no one moved to get up. Instead Nicholas turned the television on. There was a "Back to the Future" marathon playing and they decided to watch it.

Trinity leaned her head on Logan's shoulder and tried to keep her eyes open. But after he put his arm around her she quickly fell asleep.

She was aware that she was dreaming, but it was a nice dream. She was wandering through the Louvre looking at paintings with Logan by her side. Suddenly she realized she had wandered off and lost Logan. She ran frantically through the deserted halls looking for him.

"Logan!" she called out.

No response. The halls were empty. She was alone.

One of the paintings caught her attention. In the painting shadowy figures that looked like demons fell from heaven to a dark round circle. She was mesmerized.

"It didn't happen like that," Roan whispered in her ear.

Startled, she turned and saw him standing behind her, leaning over her left shoulder.

"What? The fall from heaven?" she asked.

The appearance of Roan in her dreams did not frighten her anymore. Instead, they made her curious where the dream would go.

"Yes," he answered. "The fall, when a third of the angels were cast from heaven by the big Mr. Goody Two-shoes."

"So what was it like?" she asked.

He sneered.

"Oh please. Don't tell me you can't tell me," she said, exasperated.

"Sorry Pet, I can't tell you," he said, with a wry grin.

She rolled her eyes.

"Oh, don't roll your eyes at me, Pet."

She glared at him.

"It makes me crazy," he offered.

"Well that's not a stretch for you," she said, dryly.

"Ohhhh," he drooled. "Are you being playful, Pet?"

"Nope."

"Ah, I think you were," he teased, grinning.

"Ok Roan, why are you here?"

He threw his arm over her shoulder. She looked at his arm disgusted and sighed. He steered away from the painting, his stride long and casual. They stopped in front of another painting. This one had little fat cherubs in it.

"Hmmm…how did so many artists get cherub angels so wrong?" he mused.

"Oh. They aren't chubby, baby looking angels?" she asked, joking.

"You ever seen one, Pet?" he asked, his arm still around her shoulders.

"Nope."

"They are fierce," he said.

"What do they look like?" she asked.

"Sorry, can't tell you that, Pet."

She rolled her eyes.

"Ack!" he said, shaking his finger at her. "No rolling your eyes. You don't want me to lose control do you?"

She stared at him.

"Or maybe you do," he mused.

He backed her up against the wall.

"Come on Roan, time's up," Trinity said, suddenly trying to force herself to wake up.

"Oh, don't go," he whined. "I like our times together."

"Well that's one of us," she said.

Roan leaned in to give her a kiss on the cheek. She jerked back disgusted.

"Until next time," he said.

Trinity gasped and sat straight up on the couch.

"It's okay. You're okay," Logan said, calming her down.

She realized it was a dream. She had known it was a dream, but it felt so real. She was sure Roan knew about the dream. She even wondered if her dreams were moments in an alternate reality or moments in another realm.

"Do you want to talk about it?" Logan said, quietly.

She shook her head. "It's not a big deal."

Sam was staring at her. She gave him a half-smile.

When the second "Back to the Future" movie started they ordered take-out. There was a local Chinese place that delivered. Trinity snuggled with Logan for the next movie. About halfway through, the food was delivered and everyone devoured sweet and sour pork, hot and sour soup, egg rolls, beef with broccoli, and General Tso's chicken.

Everyone opened their fortune cookies.

"You will find great fortune in your future," Nicholas read.

Everyone smiled.

167

"The one you want is right in front of you," Sam read, and blushed.

"Okay Logan, what does your say?" Trinity asked.

"Your stars are about to align."

He laughed because nobody really understood what that meant.

"Okay, you're next," Sam said, looking at Trinity.

"You are the chosen one," Trinity read aloud.

They stared at her in silence.

"Oh come on guys," she groaned. "What is that supposed to mean?"

Sam gave Logan a look. Trinity saw it.

"No. No. I saw that," she said, pointing at the two angels in her family room. "What was that about?"

They both laughed, nervously.

"Nothing," Logan assured her, grinning from ear to ear.

Trinity stared at him, unbelieving.

Logan playfully pushed her. "Relax," he said in a goofy voice.

Trinity let it go.

They spent the rest of the evening finishing the movie series. "Die Hard" was next. It was definitely a day for doing nothing but resting after a long weekend. It felt good.

Still, Trinity felt like something was amiss. She enjoyed being with Logan, but her feelings were changing. That was something she thought could never happen. Her feelings for Logan had changed from infatuation to admiration and friendship. The only thing she knew for sure, was that she wasn't sure.

She needed time. She needed to think about it, perhaps even talk to Logan when she was ready. She was a teenager. Logan was her first real crush.

For now, she would just concentrate on her upcoming performance at Stonehenge. She still needed to figure out her role in this battle between good and evil.

Maybe she really was the chosen one.

Chapter Twenty-Seven

The next morning there was a red rose by her bed. The note read, "Just because."

Trinity ran downstairs to ask Logan if he was the one sending the roses. She saw Logan's bags packed and by the front door. Concerned, she went into the kitchen and found him dressed and drinking a cup of coffee.

"Headed somewhere?" she asked him, forgetting about the rose.

"I've got to be a good nephew and go visit my aunt for a while," he said.

One of Trinity's eyebrows arched and a small grin formed at the corner of her mouth. Logan was no more a "nephew" than she was a grandma. But in front of her parents he could not exactly say, "Thousands of demons are trying to come through the portal at Stonehenge and I have to go prepare for battle." She smiled even thinking about how her parents would react.

"When will you be back?" she asked, even though she knew it was a stupid question.

Logan grinned. "Not really. Just playing it by ear. I will definitely be at your performance at Stonehenge."

Of course he would. He would be there in full Warrior Angel attire, shining like a super nova, chopping demons into pieces.

"Sam, could I talk to you for a minute?" Logan asked.

The two of them went outside for privacy. Trinity wanted to hear what they were saying. She went to the front window and peered out nonchalantly.

Logan appeared to be giving commands and Sam nodded in agreement. Then Logan leaned in and whispered fiercely to Sam who just stared at him unblinking. She flushed because she knew it was about her. She wondered if Logan was jealous. It was obvious that Sam and Trinity had grown close while Logan was away the last time.

Logan was visibly upset at Sam's response. He ran his fingers through his hair and looked worried.

"It's all up to her," she heard Sam say loudly.

Logan was not happy with that statement either. She did not know if they were talking about her relationship with Logan or the events surrounding Stonehenge.

"You have to let her chose," said Sam, loudly again. "She is a mortal and has free will."

"I guess so," Logan said, defeated.

Logan poked his finger into Sam's chest. "Take care of her. If you let something happen to her..."

Sam nodded and placed his hand on Logan's shoulder. "I got this brother."

Logan nodded; satisfied Trinity would be safe, but clearly upset at everything else.

They went back into the house. Logan said his goodbyes to the family and Trinity walked him out of the townhouse.

"Be careful," she said when she embraced him.

She pulled away and saw him grin. He had been in a thousand battles and this was just one more.

He took her face in his hands and kissed her. Trinity got an odd feeling this may be the last time she kissed him. She clung to him and pulled him close. Tears flowed down her cheeks. When they separated they were both teary-eyed.

Neither of them knew exactly what they were feeling. All the emotions surrounding the impending battle made things even more complicated.

"Don't go anywhere without Sam," Logan said.

She nodded. She knew how hard it was for Logan to make that statement.

"But...being with Sam every minute of every day is confusing me," she said, quietly. "And I think you know that."

He nodded. "It's okay. Don't be afraid of what you are feeling. Follow your heart."

That confused her even more.

"You know how I feel about you," he said. "But if you're not meant to be mine…"

"I am yours…" she interrupted, but uncertain if it was true.

"You are young, confused and unsure," he said, speaking from years of wisdom.

Trinity remembered that Logan, even though he looked like a young man, was as old as the universe. She smiled.

He hugged her one last time and backed away and was gone. Her snow angel had melted away. He was quickly becoming a memory.

She returned to the townhouse sullen. She went into the little den and sat in the window sill. She curled her knees up, wrapped her arms around herself and leaned on her chin on her knees.

"Feelings are complicated," she thought. She laughed out loud. "Even more so when there are angels involved."

She spent some time thinking about what she should do and how she felt. At some point she had grabbed a notebook and started writing lyrics. When she was done she had written three new songs.

Several hours later Sam came in and sat across from her on the window sill.

"How you feeling?" he asked.

She shrugged.

"You sad Logan is gone?"

She shrugged again.

This was not the response Sam had expected. He thought she was in here moping about Logan's departure.

"Thinking about stuff?"

She nodded.

"You'll figure it all out," he said, comforting.

She looked out the window.

Sam scooted closer. He sat cross-legged in front of her. He looked at her with puppy dog eyes. His eyes were gray today. She wondered if his eyes changed from gray to blue depending on his mood. If he was emotionally conflicted, did his eyes turn gray? If he was happy or angry were they bright blue?

"Life is gray," she said, thinking about his eyes.

Sam chuckled.

"Life is gray. It is also black and white and red and messy and emotional, mysterious, and complicated. At least your lives are. That's why we all want to be you. Did you know that? Or at least be near you," he said. "I know that I want to be near you as much as I can."

She pulled back so she could look at him. Her head swam. She knew what he wanted to tell her, but part of her did not want him to say it. She was not sure she could handle it right now. Her feelings for Logan were complex enough.

The other part of her wanted him to say it. She wanted everything to be out in the open. But she knew if he expressed his feelings for her, she would have to tell him no. She was with Logan. And she did not want to have to tell him that.

They stared at each other. Neither said a word.

"Trinity…" Sam began.

"Don't," she stopped him.

He looked at her, hurt.

"Sam, I can't."

"At least let me express my feelings. What happens from there we can figure out."

She looked out the window, pained.

"Okay," she agreed.

"I have fallen for you. I've fallen hard. Thinking about you lights up my day. Protecting you fills me with joy. I know you are with Logan. I know. But, I have to tell you how I feel so you can decide what you want to do."

She nodded, tears welling in her eyes. She did not know if she was crying because she cared for Logan or if it was because she knew she was beginning to have feelings for Sam. Or maybe both.

"I'm so confused," she said, putting her head in her hands.

Sam wrapped his brotherly arms around her.

"My dear Pal Trinity. You don't have to make any decisions. I can wait forever, literally," he smiled.

She chuckled.

He pet her head and leaned his head against her soft hair.

She cried quietly. He held her. After she regained composure she looked up, her eyes red and teary.

"I'm with Logan."

Sam bristled a little. He didn't know why, but he was not expecting that answer.

"Ok," he said, quietly.

"Are you not going to protect me anymore?" she asked, fearful.

He cupped her chin in his hand.

"I will always protect you."

She nodded.

"Can I be alone for a while?" she asked.

He nodded. She gave him a hug before he left.

"Sam," she called out when he was at the door.

He turned towards her.

"Thank you. I am honored."

He left the room. She spent more time writing and thinking. At the end of the day she felt better. Sam would be her friend and her Protector Angel. But if Sam was going to protect her, he needed to know about how much Roan was visiting her.

It was dark outside. She found the boys snacking and watching TV.

"Sam, can we go for a walk?" she asked.

He got up and they headed out the front door. They walked towards Chinatown. The Oriental street lamps were lit. There were round Chinese lanterns strung across balconies and across the street. The air smelled of roast duck and sweet and sour sauce.

She sat in a doorway. Sam followed her. The street was busier in the evening than in the day. Tourists were browsing and locals buying groceries.

"If you are going to protect me then you need to know everything that has been going on," she started.

Sam looked at her nervously. Obviously Trinity had been keeping information from him and he was not sure what she was going to say.

"Roan has visited me almost every day."

Sam looked surprised. "When? How?"

"He catches me when I'm alone somewhere. He was there in the village when we were playing capture the flag. I saw him several times each night," she explained.

"What does he say to you?" Sam asked, perturbed with himself for letting Roan get close to her.

"He is smitten with me," she said, flatly.

Sam ran his fingers through his hair and looked worried.

"What do you say to him?" Sam asked.

She shrugged.

"I find him repulsive. Roan is a demon and I and I have seen what he looks like beneath his beautiful and seductive exterior," she said. "And he tried to kill me last year."

Sam relaxed a little. "So you aren't attracted to him?"

"Heck no, his supernatural charms don't work on me."

Sam looked down the street, thinking. A Chinese lady came by on her bike and sold them some savory treats made with mysterious ingredients. They sat in silence.

"Roan is appearing in my dreams again," she said.

Sam looked at her.

"And he knows when I have the dreams and what happens in them. He taunts me with that knowledge."

Silence.

"How does he know?" she asked, bluntly. "Is it really a dream or are these things happening in another realm."

"They are dreams," Sam said. "Sort of."

"Explain."

"It's hard to explain to mortals. The workings of their minds and psyche."

"Then please explain the best you can to this mortal," she told him.

"Yes they are dreams, but obviously he is having the same dream at the same time," he said.

"But how can that be?" she asked.

"The mind is powerful, Trinity. Your mind is powerful. You have abilities you are only just beginning to discover."

"Like what?" she asked, bewildered.

"You have premonition. You dream things and then they happen. You are unaffected by Roan's touch, which is extremely rare. And you are sharing a dream with a demon. You have powers, but I don't know to what extent, yet."

She just stared at him.

"You understand? Somehow you have supernatural powers."

"Please don't tell me I'm going to grow a tail and cat ears," she joked.

"Personally I always preferred Wonder Woman to Cat Woman," he teased.

She pushed him with her shoulder and giggled.

"I'm not talking about becoming a super hero. You aren't going to start flying or turning green. But humans only use a small

178

percentage of their brain. There are the occasional few that access more of their potential. Those few are capable of amazing things."

Trinity bit her red lip. Sam poked her cheek. She grinned and poked his dimple.

"Hi," he said.

She giggled. "Hi."

Sam stood up, put out his hand and pulled her up. He put his hands on her shoulders protectively.

"Don't worry. I am not going to let you out of my sight."

She blushed.

"I'm going to need to shower once in a while," she teased.

"W-e-l-l," Sam said, stretching out the word. "I'll let you shower every now and then. Just when you start to stink."

"If it's the only time I'm alone, Roan may visit me there."

Sam glared at her.

"He better not. I will bust down the door, whether you're in your Wonder Woman Underoos or not."

She laughed. "Cat Woman."

They walked home under the Chinese lanterns. Each one glowed in the dark, like a beacon of hope.

Chapter Twenty-Eight

Several days past and Roan never appeared. On a sunny Saturday, Nicholas, Trinity and Sam browsed a street market. Trinity went into a sweets shop to get some chocolate while Sam and Nicholas continued looking through some old book on a table set up on the side walk.

Trinity was looking at all the delicious truffles in the glass case.

"Hiya Pet," Roan crooned.

Trinity was startled. It had been over a week since she had seen or heard from him. The last time, it was in a dream where they were both at the Louvre in Paris.

"I enjoyed our dream date in Paris," he said with a wicked grin.

Roan leaned on the glass case and stared at Trinity.

"It wasn't a date and I didn't enjoy it," she retorted.

"Ah, don't be that way, Pet," he smirked. "You ever wonder why you and I can both see your dreams?" he asked, appealing to her curiosity.

"Sure," she said.

"Why do you think it is?" he asked.

"I don't know and I don't care," Trinity bluffed.

"Liar," he grinned. "You're dying to know."

"Not from you," she answered. "You wouldn't tell me the truth anyway."

With that, she turned abruptly and left the candy shop. Roan did not follow. She did not know if she should tell Sam or not. It was not like she was in danger anyway with Sam just a few feet away. She decided to let this one go.

They sat outside at a pub and ordered "fish and chips." They were startled when an extra chair was plopped across the table from them and Roan sat down.

"Hello there," he said, as if they had been expecting him.

"Roan," Sam growled. "Leave now."

Roan grinned. "Oh you don't mean that."

Nicholas was dumbfounded. "You've got some nerve."

Roan signaled to the waitress.

"Hey Hun, I'll take the chicken pot pie and a soda."

"You're not eating with us," Trinity blurted, bewildered.

181

"Of course I am, Pet."

The waitress brought his soda.

Trinity stared wide-eyed at him and then at Sam. Sam looked at Roan, then at her.

"So what is it you want?" Sam asked.

"To socialize, have lunch, chit chat," Roan said, sipping his ice tea.

"Chit chat?" Trinity asked sarcastically. "Seriously?"

"Yes, Pet. Love the outfit by the way," he said, looking her up and down ogling her.

Trinity was wearing black leather leggings with zippers along the legs and knees. She wore a shredded black shirt, off the shoulder with a red tube top underneath. Her nails were black and she wore a gray beanie with her unruly, black hair down her back.

"So...you excited about your concert at Stonehenge?" Roan asked, casually, as if the conversation was completely normal.

She just stared at him. He grinned, amused at her baffled stare.

"Hey kids!" Trinity's parents called out to them as they approached.

Roan stood up and turned towards them.

"Mr. & Mrs. Heart, what a pleasure to finally meet you," he said, offering his hand. "I go to school with Trinity and Nicholas."

Trinity watched aghast that her parents were shaking hands with a Dark One.

"Trinity, your friends are all so polite and well-mannered, it's quite refreshing," Mrs. Heart said.

Trinity stifled a grimace and rolled her eyes. She did not know what to do.

"Why don't you join us all for dinner later at our town-house," Mr. Heart offered to Roan.

Before Trinity could protest, Roan spoke up. "That would be wonderful. Thank you."

Trinity shot a look at Sam and Sam just nodded in return. He wanted to see where this would go. He wanted to see what Roan wanted.

At that point there was nothing anyone could say without sounding rude. How do you tell your parents that your teenage schoolmate is really a demon that tried to kill you last winter?

"Well then, we shall see you all later tonight," her parents said as they walked off hand-in-hand.

"That was smooth," Trinity said, disgusted.

Roan grinned. "I aim to please, Pet."

She rolled her eyes.

"So, where were we?" he asked. "Ah yes…your concert at Stonehenge."

"What about it?"

"You looking forward to it?"

"None of your business."

"Ah, don't be so rude. I'm making polite conversation," Roan whined, playfully watching Sam from the corner of his eye.

"None of your business," she said again, forcefully.

Roan got up and leaned over her seat, his hands on the arms of her chair.

"I'm being nice here, Pet..." he began, in a threatening voice.

Before he could finish his sentence Sam was out of his seat and had Roan's arm in his grip.

"Back away Roan," he said, with authority. It was taking all of his patience to allow Roan even near Trinity. But he had a reason to let this encounter continue. He needed to find out what Roan was up to.

Trinity heard a bone break in Roan's arm and saw Roan wince from Sam's grip. He pulled his arm away and sat back down leaning in his chair, visibly in pain.

"Well, well, isn't this a fun dynamic," Roan said through gritted teeth.

The food came and Trinity was glad for the distraction.

"What are you doing here?" Nicholas asked Roan. "Really."

He shrugged.

"If you lay one hand, fang, or talon on Trinity I will kill you, that is if Sam doesn't beat me to it," Nicholas threatened.

"That was so last school year," Roan said, with a sly grin. "I don't want to harm Trinity."

"Then what do you want with me?" she asked, with too much desperation in her voice.

"That's for us to discuss in private...without all the body guards," he said nodding at Sam and Nicholas.

"Well that's not going to happen," said Sam.

"Hmmm....we will see about that," Roan replied.

After lunch everyone got up. Trinity did not know what to do with Roan. He was hanging out with them like they were all friends.

Roan threw his arm around Trinity.

"Where too, Pet?"

Sam instantly was in Roan's face and pushed him back into a brick wall. Again Trinity heard bones crack under the force of Sam's strength.

"You don't get to touch her, Roan. Are we clear?" Sam said, his eyes flashing. "You are lucky I am letting you live."

Roan nodded with respect. Then he grinned even though he feared Sam. "Chill, amigo."

"We're not friends. We're enemies." Sam was all business. He pressed Roan harder into the wall.

Roan gasped for air, then put his hands up, surrendering and smiled. "Sorry Pet," he groaned.

"Roan…leave," Sam said, releasing his grip.

"Fine. See you later, Pet." Roan grinned, gave Trinity a wink and walked away.

"What does he want?" Trinity almost yelled, exasperated.

"Let's just enjoy the afternoon," Nicholas said.

"I have to get to practice," Trinity said, disappointed.

"I'll come with you," Sam said. "Roan has some guts showing up like this, but we are in public so he knows I won't break him in half in front of a hundred witnesses."

Nicholas split off and went home. Trinity met her band to run through the songs they were considering for the competition. She had a couple new songs and wanted to try them out.

When they got to the studio space where they practiced Trinity introduced her new song to her band. Trinity sat on a stool and began singing. Sam watched her from the back of the room.

He immediately knew the song was about Logan.

She sang about being confused, seeking answers and finding none. Sam had seen her write those lyrics in the window sill the day Logan left. He knew the songs were not completely personal, but they were a glimpse into Trinity's soul. Sam stood entranced by Trinity's voice. She had a way of captivating her audience because she was vulnerable; she shared her soul when she was on stage.

He could not take his eyes off her. She glanced at him, saw him staring and blushed. He smiled at her. She looked down and continued singing.

Trinity practiced for two hours then walked back to the townhouse for dinner.

"That was an amazing song," Sam told Trinity, walking in the front door.

He was cut short by the sight of Roan sitting in the living room chatting with Trinity's parents. Nicholas looked relieved to see Sam.

"Roan what are you doing here?" Trinity asked, startled.

"Honey, we invited him to dinner, remember?" her mom said.

"Yes but..." she did not know how to finish.

"Hey Trinity, did your practice go well?" Roan asked, like a perfect gentleman.

"Ya sure," she said. "I'm going to go set the table."

"Let me help," Sam said, following her.

Over the table they whispered to each other.

"I thought he would not show up," she said, hoarsely. "Especially after what happened this afternoon."

"Me too," Sam said, annoyed. "I will deal with him later."

They set the table in silence. Trinity kept glancing at Roan who smiled at her every time she looked at him.

"Can you get rid of him?" Trinity whispered to Sam.

"I can't exactly whip out my sword and engage him in a heavenly battle in front of your parents."

Trinity sighed. She knew he was right. For the time being, they were stuck with him.

"I'm as curious as you are," said Sam. "Let's see what he wants."

Trinity's mom called everyone to the table. Roan took a seat next to Trinity, which put Sam and Nicholas across the table and her parents on either end. Dinner conversation was friendly, but forced. Roan asked Trinity's parents polite questions and spoke of their school days as if it was a fond memory. Trinity was disgusted.

After dinner Trinity's dad shook Roan's hand.

"It was a pleasure having dinner with your family," Roan said.

"You're welcome anytime," her dad said.

"Trinity, walk me out?" Roan asked.

There was not much she could do. If she refused, her parents would think she was rude. Roan seemed to be on his best behavior. She did not really fear that he would hurt her…at least not right now.

The two of them went outside.

"See that wasn't painful?" Roan teased.

"What are you doing?" she said, exasperated. "Why are you here? Why are you following me?"

Roan got serious and took a step closer to her. He gently took her hand and brushed her knuckles with his thumb.

"Why is it okay for them to fall for you, but not me?" he asked.

She stared at him blankly.

Roan looked down at their touching hands.

"Trinity I've fallen for you," he whispered. "This fallen angel has fallen for you."

She pulled her hand away, but gently this time.

"Roan I don't believe you."

He held her face with his hands. His finger brushing her lips. "It's true."

She backed away from his touch.

"Roan, you are a demon," said Trinity. "You tried to kill me. I could never love you."

He stepped closer. "I was an angel once," he whispered. "Just like Logan and Samuel. We were the same."

Her head was spinning.

"Trinity, Logan and I are not so different," said Roan. "We are both servants of our masters. We both do violence to our enemies. When I first met you, it was just another job. You were just another human. But knowing you has changed me. You, you have changed me."

Trinity began to tremble. "Roan, you chose evil. You made your choice."

"Is there no forgiveness for a fallen angel?" he asked. "A human can make mistake after mistake and he is forgiven. But what about me? Is forgiveness too much to ask for a reformed fallen angel?"

He was pleading with her. Trinity saw a single tear trace down his face and fall to the ground.

"Take that up with your Maker," Trinity said, not knowing the answer.

"Do you believe I am all evil?" he asked.

"I don't know," she answered, honestly.

She immediately knew her answer was a mistake. A sly grin slipped across Roan's face and she regretted admitting that out loud. She had shown weakness.

"I have to go," she said swiftly, and went inside the house.

Roan sauntered down the street, whistling one of Trinity's songs.

Chapter Twenty-Nine

Trinity dreamed that night.

She wore a black tulle skirt, black corset, and black and white striped thigh-high socks. Her hair was gathered into two messy knots that hung either side of the base of her neck. She had on a petite, red, top hat, tilted off the side of her head. She wore heavy black eyeliner and cherry red lipstick.

It was night. She stood in front of a large circus tent. She heard music from inside the tent. It sounded like *Secret Door* by Evanescence. She was to look inside the tent, but she was unsure. She hesitated.

Finally gathering courage, she stepped into the circus tent. Inside, streamers of rich, colored fabric draped from the center of

190

the dome to the edges. Hundreds of twinkle lights were draped around the tent, illuminating it with drama and mystery.

Aerial silk acrobats tumbled down from the ceiling. She gasped. They gracefully performed a routine in perfect unison. She watched in wonder. Cirque du Soleil type characters pranced around the tent. All the performers were aware of her presence. It was as if they were performing for her.

She wandered among the prancing characters, running her hand over the silky streamers. Performers swarmed about her. Acrobats, jugglers, a maze of mystery and enchantment.

The music intensified and the performers moved in a frenzy with the music. She felt disoriented. She felt lost. She fought to find her way back to the entrance, but the door was gone. She panicked. The music grew more frantic, the performers moved even faster, and their faces began to change. Rather than beautiful and exotic, they were now gruesome and hideous. Every one of the acrobats was a demon. Leathery wings sprouted from their backs. Fangs and jaws of sharp teeth grew from their once perfect mouths. Each one transformed into something different. They clawed at her skirt. They ripped her stockings, pulled her hair and scratched her arms and shoulders. She ran but could not find an escape.

She turned to push away a demon that pulled on her hair.

SLAM! She ran into someone and screamed in fright. When she looked up to see who held her firmly, it was Roan. He was dressed in a gothic tuxedo and black top hat. He looked like a ringmaster.

"It's okay, Pet," he crooned. "I will protect you."

191

She did not know if she should run from him or stay in the solace of his arms. She stood frozen, looking at him.

"I have control over all of them," he said soothingly. "I can protect you from them."

He yelled at the demonic performers, "Away!"

Instantly they all disappeared. The music changed to a sweet lullaby. Roan held her in his arms and looked down at her. He gently rocked her back and forth.

"See, Pet…all gone."

She slowly backed away from him.

"No," she said, softly.

"No?" he asked, confused.

"No. I don't believe you."

A wicked grin crossed Roan's face.

"You are too smart for you own good, aren't you?" he asked, cruelly.

"Leave me, Roan," she said, sternly.

"No!" he said, mocking her and swaggered toward her.

She took another step back.

"Roan, leave me," she warned, again.

"Mmmm…are you going to get feisty, Pet?"

She turned to run but before she could Roan had her in his arms. He grabbed her hair and pulled her head back, forcing her to look into his eyes.

"T…R…I…N…I…T…Y," he whispered, drawing out her name.

"RUN!" he commanded, pushing her away from him.

192

She took off running across the tent and out into the night. A vast field was in front of her and she sprinted as fast as she could. Roan was close behind, salivating at the prospect of catching his prey.

Trinity stopped suddenly, turned and faced Roan. He came to a sudden about ten feet away from her.

"Please help me," she prayed. "Please help me."

Roan looked worried. He stared at Trinity then glanced nervously left and right. He began backing up and stepped into Sam, who was suddenly standing right behind him. Sam shone brightly like a star. His muscles rippled and he held a sword in his hand.

Trinity sucked in her breath. Sam looked…she found no words to describe it.

"She said leave her," Sam said, sternly shoving Roan to the ground.

Roan cowered. "Don't hurt me," he sniveled.

"Be gone!" Sam yelled, his voice reverberating like thunder.

Sam lifted his sword above his head and brought it down with a mighty force. Trinity saw a split second of terror in Roan's face, just before Sam's sword touched his brow. Then Roan vanished and Sam's sword buried halfway to the hilt in the ground where Roan was only seconds before.

Trinity crumpled to her knees. Sam rushed to her side and held her.

"I was deceived," she said, tearfully.

"It's okay," Sam soothed. "It's what they do. They appeal to whatever part of you that will accept them and prey upon that weakness."

She sniffled. "You came."

"I will always come, Trinity."

She stared at him.

"It's who I am; I protect, I defend, I rescue," he said, matter-of-factly without any ego.

She smiled and closed her eyes.

They both sighed deeply. He poked her cheek. She stifled a chuckle. He was playful, even at time like this. She liked that about him.

"Night night Sammy."

She closed her eyes and drifted off a dreamless sleep.

Chapter Thirty

Sam went out early to grab a coffee for Trinity. As he rounded the corner onto Shaftsbury he nearly ran into Roan who was leaning against a brick building waiting for him.

"You thought you were pretty slick horning in for dinner didn't you," Sam said, angrily.

Roan shrugged.

"Stay away from her, Roan," Sam warned and started to walk away.

'You have feelings for her, don't you?" Roan yelled after him.

Sam turned. "So what."

"She is amazing," Roan said, acknowledging how Sam could fall for her. "But she isn't choosing you, is she?"

Sam looked away. He ran his hands through his unruly blonde hair.

"It doesn't matter," Sam said, and turned to walk away again.

"What if you could have her?" Roan asked. "What would you do to make Trinity chose you?"

Sam turned to Roan and took a step closer. "She's human. She has free will."

"Meh." Roan murmured. "There are ways around that."

"I wouldn't do that to her," Sam said, firmly.

"She would be yours. She would love you. You could live happily ever after," Roan crooned, stepping towards Sam.

Sam hesitated.

"Who knows where you will be dispatched to next. You could never see her again," Roan said, sensing that Sam was weakening.

Sam sighed.

"Samuel, think this through carefully," said Roan. "You could leave all this. You could take her and see the world with her. You wouldn't have to worry about Stonehenge, it wouldn't be your problem anymore. Just fall with me. I will give you what your heart wants most."

Sam ran his hand through his hair again. "No," he said, shakily.

"Sam. Think about it."

Sam sighed.

"No. Roan. No. I won't fall. I won't betray my Maker," Sam said, confidently.

"Not even for her?"

"No!" Sam yelled, sternly. "I won't do it."

Roan cowered at Sam's voice and disappeared. He had tried. He might try again. He needed to find a chink in Trinity's armor. He needed to do everything it took to keep Trinity away from Stonehenge. He would have to try something else.

Sam continued on his way to get coffee.

Trinity awoke and remembered her dream. This dream was different from all the rest. Roan wasn't trying to carry her off, he wanted a chase. This wasn't a premonition. This was more like an ordinary dream, a dream that Roan interrupted. Trinity wondered what it meant.

She could not find Sam. She walked through the entire townhouse. She pushed her brother's door open. He was on his bed reading.

"Have you seen Sam?" she asked.

Nicholas shrugged.

Trinity went to the front door, looked out. Nothing. She went back inside and sat on a kitchen barstool. It was odd that Sam would leave without saying anything. Just as she was about to look through the house again Sam came through the front door with coffee in hand.

She sighed with relief.

"Here you go Pal Trinity. Thought you might want some coffee this morning," he said, cheerfully, with a cute grin.

She took the coffee and poked his dimple.

"Thanks Pal Sam."

Trinity had a serious look on her face.

He sat next to her on the barstool. He leaned his shoulder against hers and gave her a cheesy grin for effect.

She laughed.

"And there's that beautiful smile," he said, in a sweet voice.

She took a sip of coffee.

"I have an idea," he began, "since you are stuck with me, let me plan our day."

She grinned. She kinda liked that idea. Good surprises were always fun. She agreed to let him plan the day's activities.

"Ok. After our coffee, go get dressed and we will head out," Sam said, excited.

They sipped their coffee. Trinity debated whether or not to tell Sam about her dream. She decided she would later. Right now they were in such a good mood, she did not want to ruin it. After coffee, Trinity ran up to get dressed. She bound down the stairs wearing black shorts, thigh-highs scrunched around her knees, combat boots and a black and white-striped, fitted T-shirt. She wore her hair in two braids.

"You look scrumptious," he teased.

"Scrumptious, eh? What am I, a crumpet?" she asked.

He poked her cheek and pulled on one of her braids, keeping the mood light.

"So what are we doing Pal Sammy?" she asked.

"First, we are going to go to the Natural History Museum," he said.

Trinity brightened up. She had not been there yet, but she had wanted to go and see the dinosaur skeletons. They took the tube to the museum. The first thing they looked at was the half-buried skeleton of an Edmontosaurus. Its tail was missing and it was assumed that a predator ate it.

Trinity leaned on the glass and stared.

"This is amazing," she said. "What was it like when dinosaurs roamed the earth?"

Sam looked at her and smiled.

"You aren't going to tell me, are you?" she asked.

"Some things are meant to remain a mystery."

"Oh come on. I have access to someone who was alive when dinosaurs roamed the earth and you won't tell me anything?" she whined.

She grabbed his arm with both of her hands and yanked.

"Come on, Pal Sammy. Just tell me about the T-Rex," she pleaded.

"They were majestic and fierce and that is all I am going to tell you," he said, grinning.

"Oh, come on," she said. "I could get that much from reading the little sign."

She was so cute, he almost could not refuse. But he knew that it was not his place to tell her about the past. Humans had to discover and unravel mysteries for themselves.

They looked at the Triceratops exhibit. An animal that massive was impressive. Trinity and Sam continued to walk through the museum. Each time they viewed another exhibit Trinity begged Sam to tell her more than the informational panels revealed. Each time, Sam refused.

"How are you feeling?" Sam asked, watching her carefully.

All that Trinity had been through was more than most humans could emotionally deal with, and yet she seemed to be thriving.

"I'm good," she said.

"But…" he said.

"I'm just not sure what is going to happen at Stonehenge and that scares me," she said.

"That's understandable."

Silence.

"I will be with you every moment," he assured her.

"You will have hundreds of demons to deal with. I'm not so sure you can protect me with so much going on," she said, fearing he would be offended.

"My one job at Stonehenge is to protect you," he explained. "I'm not like Logan, whose job is to fight the forces that come through the portal."

Trinity bit her lip and stood face-to-face with him.

"You promise you won't leave me?" she asked, worried.

He took her face in his hands.

"I will be by your side every second. I will not leave you alone."

She stared at him, her brow furrowed.

"I would never forgive myself if something happened to you," he whispered.

"But there will be so many of them," she said, softly.

He grinned.

"Demons fear me," he said, confidently. "Don't they?"

He grinned, knowing Trinity had seen Roan cower before him.

She smiled and took a step back.

"Roan sure does."

She leaned in close and whispered in his ear, "You let something happen to me and I will come back and haunt you the rest of your life."

Sam's laughter shattered the silence of the museum, drawing stares.

"Shhh," she warned.

"Let's go get some food, Pal Trinity."

Sam took her to a little Moroccan restaurant hidden on a side street. They sat cross-legged on pillows on the floor. There were Berber rugs on the floors and the walls were covered with tapestries. The ceilings look like a linen tent. Colored lanterns added to the exotic mystique.

"So what do you think will be your major at Oxford?" Sam asked.

"I've been interested in music. They have an amazing music department. I'd like to compose," she said between bites.

"That definitely seems to fit you. You are a very talented composer."

Trinity sipped her mint tea and smiled. College was going to be an exciting new adventure. She wondered how her angel boyfriend was going to fit into college life. Could there really be a future with an angel? Or was it just a fantasy. How could they ever live a normal life?

They were silent while Trinity mulled over her thoughts.

"Once the battle at Stonehenge is over, will you be leaving?" Trinity asked, not wanting to hear the answer.

He smiled at her, not sure what to say.

"I don't know," he finally answered.

"Is Logan going back to Shadowland Academy this fall?" she asked.

"Probably not," Sam said, trying to read her face.

"So I am alone," she said, quietly.

"You are never alone."

"But you won't be there. Logan won't be there. Roan isn't going to leave me alone you know."

"I won't let Roan hurt you," Sam said.

She was not convinced. This coming school year was starting to worry her. How could she do it without Logan or Sam? She needed them near. Not just to protect her, but to be her friends. After everything she had experienced the past year, she didn't think human friends could fill the void. She knew too much. To bear the secrets of all she had experienced would be too heavy a burden without friends who understood.

She bristled, trying to prepare herself for the idea that in a few weeks this wonderful friendship could be over. Sam noticed her body stiffen and the frown on her face.

"Trinity, you aren't going to lose me," Sam said, quietly.

She snapped out of her daze.

"How so?" she asked.

"I'm not going to let the end of the summer be the end of our friendship."

"But if you have to leave, then what can you do about it?" she asked.

"I don't know right now. But, I'm not going to leave you forever. There may be a period when I can't be here, but I will come back to you."

Trinity wasn't sure how to feel. She was conflicted.

"I promise. I will come back."

She did not know if Sam's dedication made her happy, or if she'd rather hear it from Logan. Or maybe neither. Or both. Yes, she was confused.

"I have one more surprise for you today," he told her.

She grinned.

"What is it?" she asked.

"Come with me." he said as he led her from the restaurant.

They walked together down Shaftesbury towards the Queens Theater.

"Oh no...you didn't!" she exclaimed, as they approached the theater.

"I did," he said, grinning.

He showed her the theater tickets. Les Miserable.

Trinity skipped with glee. She had wanted to see the musical for such a long time, but they had not been able to get tickets. She leaped at Sam, wrapped her arms around him and gave him a big hug.

He sighed. She felt good. She felt right. He did not want to keep his feelings in check. He wanted to be able to hold her anytime he wanted. She was still Logan's girlfriend. He respected her decision but he did not want to give up. What guy gave up pursuing the girl he cared for?

Trinity dragged him to the entrance. He handed the custodian their tickets and they found their seats. Perfect seats.

When the lights dimmed she clasped her hands together, delighted. Sam looked longingly at her hand. He wanted to hold it.

Trinity barely moved the entire program. He caught her holding her breath during several of the songs. He had to lean over a few times and whisper, "Breathe."

She gave him a silly grin and took a breath.

When it was over she stood and enthusiastically applauded the cast. When everyone was filing out of the theater she jumped up and down and hugged Sam.

"Thank you!" she exclaimed, giddy. "That was amazing."

She skipped through the front doors of the theater out into the crisp night air. She turned back to Sam.

"Oh I can't even think about going to sleep!" she said, grinning from ear to ear.

"Let's just walk slowly back towards the townhouse," he suggested.

She grinned. People were pouring out of the theater. The streets were alive. A theater down the street was letting out about the same time and everyone was buzzing with excitement.

Trinity skipped down the street, twirling like a little girl. Sam watched with a smile. She was so happy. He loved seeing her like this. His feelings were overwhelming. He needed to tell her, but he was not sure he should.

When they got near the townhouse Sam grabbed her around the waist in the middle of one of her twirls catching her off guard. She giggled. He pulled her close. He could not help himself. He lost control.

"I think I love you, Trinity," he whispered, before he could catch himself.

Instantly, she was serious. No more laughter. She stopped moving. She stood in his arms. She did not know what to say. He should not have said it. She was just a teenager. What did she know about love? When someone who actually lives forever tells you they will love you forever, it is intimidating. Especially for a mortal.

"Sam…" she started, seriously.

She did not know what to say. He had previously told her that he was falling for her. A crush was one thing, but "love" was a completely different matter. To make things worse, she already told him she chooses Logan. Why did he not respect that and not push it any further.

"I…I'm with Logan," was all she could say.

"You can't say you don't feel anything for me," he plead, desperately. "I see it in your eyes."

"Sam…I'm not going to talk about this right now," she said backing away. "It's not right."

"Just give me some hope that maybe, maybe someday you could feel for me like I feel for you," he said, needing a glimmer of hope.

"Sam," she whispered. "I can't."

She took her head into her hands and whimpered. It was not supposed to be like this. She needed to sort out her feelings first. She needed to talk to Logan. Why did Sam have to say that right now?

"Trinity, I just want to know if there is hope," he begged.

"Sam," she said, a tear running down her cheek. "I can't answer."

She grew angrier and upset. Even after their last conversation Sam pressed the issue. She had been clear with him. They were just friends. They could only be friends.

"Why'd you say that? Why'd you say that right now?" she asked, crying angrily.

Their beautiful day together was ruined. She ran into the townhouse, threw herself onto the bed and cried herself to sleep.

Sam ran his hand through his blonde, unruly hair. He had ruined everything. It had been such a perfect day and he had thrown it all away. He lost control of his emotions for the first time ever. He was angry with himself.

He clenched his fists and let roar with a primal scream. "Ahhhh!" The force of his voice shattered a neighbor's window and set off a car alarm.

Sam ran down the street away from the townhouse. He did not know what to do. He did not know how to feel. He slowed down and turned into a dark alley. He leaned against the brick wall and slumped down to the pavement, his head in his hands.

He cried.

"You okay?" he heard a voice.

He looked up. Roan was standing over him, a hood pulled over his head. Roan slid down the brick wall and sat next to down next to Sam.

"Roan, leave me alone," he said, half-heartedly.

"I tried to help you Samuel. I tried to give you her love," Roan said, quietly. "I just want to see you happy. I want to see her happy."

Sam looked at him and rolled his eyes.

"Come on Samuel, I admit it, I've become a big softy. That girl has changed me," said Roan.

"That girl has changed all of us," Sam said.

"I don't know what it is about her, Sam, but I want her to be happy," Roan said. "The girl has wrapped me around her finger."

Sam knew the feeling. He wanted with all his heart for Trinity to love him back.

"Sam, my offer still stands. You can have her love."

Sam stared off into the distance. He was tempted by the offer. He wanted Trinity to love him. He could feel a powerful urge to fall.

"I can't," Sam said, unconvincingly.

"You really need to think about this, Sam," Roan crooned. "Think about her in your arms whenever you want. Logan would be out of the picture. She would be all yours."

Sam closed his eyes. The temptation was too strong. He wanted to fall. He wanted her.

I will do it, thought Sam. I will fall and be with Trinity.

Instead, he said out loud, "Not tonight."

Roan placed his hand on Sam's shoulder, "You sure?"

Sam nodded with his head in his hands.

Roan knew his window of opportunity had passed. He left Sam sitting in the alley.

Sam sat for several more minutes before returning to the townhouse. He slipped in quietly and crawled into bed. He dreamed of Roan and having Trinity all to himself.

Chapter Thirty-One

Trinity woke up in her clothes. She changed into sweats and a T-shirt. She washed her face and sat in the window sill. She did not know what to say to Sam. She did not want to lose his friendship but they could not have the relationship that he wanted. They had to be just friends. She did not want to give him false hope, especially when she was confused about her own feelings.

She went downstairs. Sam was in the kitchen with Nicholas. She ignored him. She did not know what to say. She avoided eye contact with him. She made herself some toast. She grabbed a napkin.

"I'm going out today. See you guys later," she said, dashing out the door before anyone could stop her.

209

She almost ran down the street in fear Sam would follow her out the door. He did, he ran after her. He was upset. Rather than talk about what happened last night she wanted to run away from it. He was angry.

"Trinity stop!" he almost ordered her.

Trinity stopped walking.

"I don't want to talk," she said, turning to face him.

"We need to talk about what happened last night," he said.

"What I need is time away from you," she replied.

"You aren't making this any easier," he said, angrily.

"You're the one that made it weird," she said. "Why couldn't you just leave things the way they were?"

He ran his hand through his hair roughly. "We have to talk about this."

He sounded desperate.

"Not now," she said and ran away from him.

"Trinity, you're acting like a child," he yelled after her.

She stopped and yelled back, "I am a child! You are thousands of years old and I'm only seventeen."

She ran away. She needed space and time to think. And Sam needed time to calm down and hopefully come to his senses.

Trinity spent the afternoon lazing on a patch of grass in a park, her headphones in her ears. She did not know how to sort through her feelings. Sam needed to clear his head and stop talking about "them" and concentrate on the big event at Stonehenge. Everything else could wait.

After a morning of music in her ears, she had calmed down. She was ready to go back to the townhouse. She snuck back in the house and went to her bedroom. She sat in the window sill, thinking.

There was a tentative knock on her door.

"Come in," she said.

Sam opened the door, and sat across from her in the window sill. They sat in silence for a moment. She looked at him. He was so cute, with his blue eyes and curly blonde hair. She bit her lip. She did not know how to start. He did.

"Trinity, I had an amazing time yesterday," said Sam.

She smiled. "Me too."

"I'm just really confused about…."

"Ya…I know," she said, interrupting. "But Sam, you gotta set all that aside for right now."

He looked out the window.

"There are bigger issues at hand," she continued. "When all this is over, I need to sort through my feelings. But right now, we both need to focus on this upcoming event at Stonehenge and how to survive it."

She looked at him, scooted closer till they were face to face.

"I need you to be on your A -game Sam. I need to live through this. I need you to protect me."

He looked down at his hands. Last night he had almost let Roan talk him into falling, just so he could make Trinity love him. But Sam could not make Trinity love him. Roan was a trickster. He promised things he could not deliver.

"I know," he said, softly. "I'm sorry about last night. I shouldn't have said those things." He looked at her face, longing.

"Let's talk about all this after Stonehenge," she suggested.

He nodded.

"You realize it may not have the outcome you want. But at least then we won't be dealing with thousands of demons who want to destroy the earth," she said.

He nodded sadly.

"Arrggghhh!" she said, frustrated.

She leaned her head back.

"Is this gonna ruin the friendship we have?" she asked, sadly.

Sam poked her cheek and grinned.

"I hope not, Pal Trinity," he said, playfully.

She breathed a sigh of relief and smiled.

Chapter Thirty-two

The next day Sam told Nicholas and Trinity he was being called away for a day. Trinity looked worried.

"You will be fine," he assured her. "I will be back tomorrow. I've been ordered to go, but I will be back within twenty-four hours."

"What if something happens?" she asked.

"You know how to call for me," he said, smiling at her. "You've been fine without us before. You are strong and confident. You can handle this."

Trinity knew he was right. She had gone her entire life without "them," she could go one day without "them" now.

Sam walked out the front door and was gone. Trinity watched him go. She knew once he rounded the corner he would simply vanish into thin air. It made her smile.

She decided she needed to spend the day alone with no one around her to cloud her emotions.

Trinity wandered through London with no destination in mind. She browsed through stores and snacked on yummy food. She bought a pair of earrings she and found a cute pair of shoes. She was enjoying the alone time. Logan and Sam's presence had actually smothered her a bit. Since they liked to hover, being alone was a breath of fresh air.

With a clear head, she realized she did not know how she felt about either of them. She knew she really liked Sam. But at the same time she was torn because Logan was her first big crush. For some reason, she could not let go of that.

After thinking it through, she realized she feared breaking his heart. He was an angel. He was special. Had he ever had a broken heart? She feared how that would affect him.

Trinity walked past the Queen Theater on Shaftsbury and thought about last night. Sam had been so kind and planned such a wonderful day for the two of them. She smiled thinking about it. She stood across the street from the theater, her arms wrapped around herself.

Last night would have been perfect if Sam had been free to kiss her. But he could not. He had expressed his feelings for her and it ended in a disaster. She hoped they would be able to move

214

forward and deal with the impending battle at Stonehenge. Right now, that was more important than any crush.

She walked down the street toward her townhouse. She knew what she needed to do. She just was not sure about the timing. She would wait until after Stonehenge.

Trinity skipped through the front door of their house and came to an abrupt stop. Roan was sitting in her kitchen on a barstool chatting with her dad. The two of them were laughing like old friends.

"Hey Hun, look who I ran into today," her dad said, gesturing towards Roan.

"Hey Trinity," Roan said, smiling.

Trinity slowly made her way into the kitchen.

"Hi Roan," she said, shortly. "What are you doing here?"

"Your dad invited me," Roan said smiling at Mr. Heart.

"Ah," was all Trinity could muster.

Flashing through her mind were images of Roan devouring her family. She was pretty sure Roan could see fear in her eyes. He gave her a reassuring smile. He would not be devouring her family…today.

"I need to take this stuff up stairs," she said and ran off.

She stopped by Nicholas' bedroom. He was on his bed reading.

"You know there is a demon in our kitchen?" she asked, sarcastically.

"Yup."

"And…"

"And what?" he asked, without looking up from his book.

"What are we going to do?" she asked, exasperated.

"Don't provoke him?"

Trinity rolled her eyes. "So we are just gonna serve up our best food and entertain him?"

"Well, you know that verse about entertaining angels unaware?" Nicholas said, continuing to read his book. "Well Dad is entertaining a demon unaware."

Trinity huffed off to her room. When she came back by to go downstairs she stopped again at Nicholas door.

"You coming downstairs?" she asked.

"Nope," he said, dryly.

"So I have to keep my eye on Roan by myself?" she asked, perturbed.

"Yup."

Trinity ran over and jumped on Nicholas. She jumped up and down on his bed.

"Can you read with me jumping up and down like this?" she asked, playfully.

Nicholas kept reading.

"Yup."

She made the mattress jump up and down. Nicholas was being tossed to and fro.

"Can you keep reading now?" she asked, with a satisfied grin.

Nicholas kept reading his book even though the pages were jumping around.

"You can't jump forever," he said smugly.

She leaped on top of him and grabbed his book.

"How about now?" she asked, holding his book out of reach.

He rolled her over and reached for his book. She kept it just out of his reach. Finally he sat on her, held her arms down and grabbed the book. He rolled over next to her and they laughed.

"Seriously though, what's the game plan?" she asked.

"Wait until he leaves," Nicholas said, shrugging.

"You are just gonna hole yourself up here till he leaves?" she asked, swatting him. "What if he devours mom and dad?"

"I'm pretty sure he just wants to devour you, Sugar lips," Nicholas said, attempting to read again.

Trinity smacked her brother hard. He winced. She rolled off the bed and went downstairs.

"Trinity, I've got a phone call to make. Why don't you entertain Roan while your mom runs out to get dinner?" her dad asked.

Trinity groaned internally.

Her dad went to his office and her mom walked out the front door to get some take-out. Roan leaned on the counter and grinned at Trinity.

"Yes Trinity, entertain me," he said, in a smoldering voice and laughed.

She rolled her eyes. She had thought about praying and calling for Sam. But decided to wait until she knew she was in danger. Maybe this time she would find out what Roan really wanted with her.

They went into the family room where Trinity plopped down on the couch. Roan sat on the ottoman, staring at her.

"What are you doing here?" she asked, perturbed.

"I ran into your dad…"

She cut him off. "Knock that off. We both know you didn't run into my dad."

He grinned.

"Your mom's cooking was so good I had to come for more?" he suggested.

"Well tonight's take-out, so I guess you can leave," she said, leaning forward.

They were face-to-face.

"I like take-out, too," he said, smugly.

She rolled her eyes.

"Ah! Don't do that, Pet," he said, with longing in his voice.

"Why?" she yelled, exasperated. "Why must I not roll my eyes?"

He leaned in until they were inches apart.

"You make me lose control," he said, seriously. The way he said it, she was instantly afraid.

"Oh," she said, quietly.

She did not want him to lose control. She knew what that looked like. It would probably end with her death. She leaned back against the couch, with a prayer on the tip of her tongue, ready to summon Sam at any moment.

"Exactly," he said, relaxing.

"So what are we supposed to do?" she asked.

"You want to play a game?" he asked.

"I don't think I like your games," she said, sourly.

He laughed.

"I mean like cards or monopoly," he said, chuckling.

"Seriously?" she asked. "We are going to sit here and play monopoly."

"Kinda silly isn't it," he said, grinning.

"Very."

She looked at him. He looked at her.

"Oh for goodness' sake," she said. "Tell me what you are doing here."

"I'm bored," he said.

"You're bored here? Or you came here because you were bored?" Trinity asked, not believing a word.

"I came here because I was bored."

"Oh, so torturing me is entertainment," she said, sourly.

"Oh hush," he said, chuckling. "This isn't torture."

"You're a demon!" she nearly yelled. "You tried to kill me last year, remember?"

She lifted up her shirt to show the where the wound had been. The angels had healed her and left a black feather tattoo in its place.

"Nice abs," he said, arching one eyebrow.

She got up and went into the kitchen. He followed her.

"You are impossible!" she said, angrily.

"No I'm not. I'm fun and mysterious and dangerous," he said, leaning over her.

219

"I'll give you dangerous," she said. "Fun? Hell no."

"Interesting choice of words, Pet," he said, sneering.

She rolled her eyes and moved away. He grabbed her and held her firmly.

"Don't roll your eyes around me, Pet. I'm not teasing about that," he said, fiercely. "I'm the demon of lust, you understand…once I lose control I can't stop."

She trembled and stood still, wide-eyed. He smelled her neck. She was frozen. Her thoughts scrambled. She could not even whisper a prayer.

"Oh, you smell so good," he drooled.

"Roan," she said, meekly.

He continued smelling her neck and hair. His cheek was touching hers.

"Roan," she whispered. "Please stop."

She closed her eyes.

He paused and looked at her standing with her eyes squeezed closed.

"Open your eyes," he said, regaining control.

She obeyed.

"You see?" he said.

She nodded silently.

"Trinity, I don't want to lose control. But I'm a fallen angel, a demon. I'm dark and twisted and evil and I could hurt you."

She nodded again. He released her and backed away.

"Tell your parents I'm sorry but I had to go," he said.

He walked out the front door. Trinity stood frozen, terrified. What was that all about?

Trinity was in her room waiting when Sam returned. He knocked on her bedroom door. She flew at him and hugged him.

"I'm so glad you are back," she said, relief washing over her.

"Anything happen while I was away?" he asked.

They both crossed to the window sill and sat.

"I came home last night and Roan was in the kitchen chatting with my dad like we were all best friends," she said, annoyed.

Sam was concerned and furrowed his eyebrow.

"Nothing much happened, "she explained. "He left before dinner."

"Don't be fooled by him," Sam warned. "He is bound to evil."

"What do you mean?" she asked.

"When the dark angels fell and chose to follow Lucifer, they were bound to evil. They were bound to serve evil. Nothing can make them good again. They aren't like humans, who get endless chances."

"So, if he wanted to be good, he couldn't?" she asked.

"Exactly," Sam confirmed.

"Could he struggle with it?" she asked. "Could he desire to be good but because he is bound to serve evil, he just can't?"

"I don't know," Sam said. "I guess it's possible. The only problem is, he absolutely cannot be good. So no matter what the struggle, in the end he will always be evil."

"Wow," she said.

"It was a choice he made when he chose to fall," Sam said.

"You wouldn't ever fall would you?" she asked, concerned.

He looked at her. His smile faltered.

"Sam?"

He looked away for a second and then back at her.

"No, I won't ever fall," he said.

She grabbed his hand and held it close to her.

"Promise me Sam. Promise me right now you will never fall."

He grinned at her and poked her cheek.

"I promise you Trinity. I will never fall," he whispered.

She breathed a sigh of relief. They sat staring at each other.

"Oh I almost forgot!" he said, excited.

"What?" she asked.

"We need to go back to Salisbury and Stonehenge," he said, grinning.

"Why?" she asked, leery. "And why are you so excited about going back there?"

"I can't tell you," he said. "You have to find out for yourself."

"Sammy, what are you up to?" she said, suspiciously.

He poked her cheek and grinned.

Chapter Thirty-Three

Trinity, Nicholas and Sam stepped off the train in Salisbury.

"So how am I supposed to find whatever it is I am supposed to find?" she asked.

"I thought we could start with the cathedral here in Salisbury," he said.

"Do you know what I am supposed to find?" she asked.

"Yes and no," he answered.

"Seriously?" she asked, dryly.

"Seriously," he said.

She pushed him playfully.

They walked a few blocks to the Salisbury Cathedral. They stepped into the main sanctuary and admired the architecture.

Sam and Nicholas ventured off to look at the Magna Carta which was kept in the Chapter House. Trinity explored the cathedral, admiring the statues and paintings. When she came to one of the chapels she saw a painting of a woman titled, "Guardian."

Trinity gasped.

When Nicholas and Sam found her she was in a trance, staring at the painting.

"What is it?" Nicholas asked, turning to look at the painting.

He gasped.

"It could almost be you," he exclaimed.

The twins stared in disbelief.

Sam looked at the painting and smiled, knowingly.

"I don't understand," she said. "Who is she?"

"She was one of the original Guardians," Sam said.

"But…" she started.

"How…" Nicholas asked.

"I don't understand," she said. "Can you explain?"

"I think you need to talk to your great-grandmother," came Logan's voice from behind her.

Trinity spun around. She was not expecting to see him here. She ran and gave him a hug. He smiled down at her.

"What are you doing here?" she asked.

"This is important," he said. "I couldn't miss this."

"What is important?" she asked, exasperated. "And who is my great-grandmother? Both of them are dead."

"You have a lot of questions and there are answers," Logan said. "But all in good time."

"No. Not all in good time!" she said, firmly. "Why does she is painting look like me?"

Logan stared at Trinity, grinning.

"I'm related to her, aren't I?" she whispered.

Logan grinned. Sam stood to the side, watching Trinity realize who she was.

"I'm a Guardian?" she asked.

"You both are," Logan said, nodding at Nicholas.

Trinity looked wide-eyed at her brother.

"You are telling me that Trinity and I are descendants of the Guardians, and therefore we are both Guardians?" he asked.

Logan nodded.

"Do our parents know about all this?" Trinity asked.

"You need to talk to your great-grandmother." Logan said, again.

"Where is she?" Trinity asked.

"Near Stonehenge," Logan said, offering his hand to Trinity. "You want to meet her?"

Trinity looked at her brother and they both nodded at Logan.

They took the bus to Stonehenge. Trinity and Nicholas were silent. This was a lot to take in.

They stepped off the bus and walked down a sheep trail. Logan held Trinity's hand and led the way. Sam and Nicholas trailed behind.

They approached a little cottage. Logan knocked on the door. No answer. He knocked again.

The door creaked opened and a little old lady with two long white braids peaked out. She wore a black shawl and had a mischievous gleam in her eye.

Trinity and Nicholas knew immediately this was their great-grandmother.

The old woman embraced them both.

"Come in. I've been waiting for you for many years," she said, smiling.

"I don't understand," Trinity said.

"I know my dearest. I will explain," the old woman said and patted the seat next to her.

Nicholas and Trinity sat.

"My name is Naomie. I am your great-grandmother," she started. "My daughter is your mother's birth mother. Your mom was adopted when she was just an infant by a nice American family, your adopted grandparents. When your mom was born, there was a surge of demons who tried to destroy an entire generation of guardians. They killed many children and infants. To protect your mother from the reach of the demons, my daughter gave her up for adoption."

Trinity was dumbfounded. She had never heard any of this. She looked at her brother, he instinctively looked at her.

Their grandmother continued.

"We lost track of her adopted family. We didn't even know she had had children of her own. Twins."

"Does my mom know she was adopted?" Trinity asked.

"I don't know," said Naomie. "That is a very delicate subject, so approach it carefully.

"So what does this mean?" Trinity asked.

Her great-grandmother smiled at her and took the twins' hands in hers.

"You both are Guardians. Very, very special Guardians."

"Why?" asked Nicholas.

"Because your birth was prophesied many years ago," Naomie said. "Long ago the key to Stonehenge was lost. This key could close the portal forever. And no demon could pass through again. We have found clues but we do not know where it is. It was prophesied that twins would be born into the Guardian family. They would find the relic, and restore the key to Stonehenge."

"You think we are the twins that were prophesied about?" Trinity asked, doubtful.

"I know you are," their great-grandmother said. "You are the first and only twins ever to be born into the Guardian family."

"So not only are we Guardians, like you, but we are special Guardians that were prophesied to come and do some great thing to protect Stonehenge?" Trinity asked, rambling.

"Yes, dear," her great-grandmother said, patting her hand. "And that key is the one relic that can lock the portal to Stonehenge forever."

"Wait, so even if the there is a huge fight and the Dark Ones are kept off the earth, they could come back?" Trinity asked.

Her great-grandmother nodded. "Unless we find the key and lock the portal. Then it will be forever closed to the Dark Ones. You and Nicholas are very powerful Guardians."

Trinity nodded her head. "I have these dreams. They come true and."

"Yes my child," said her great-grandmother. "You have special powers. Do you know why?"

"No," Trinity said, bewildered.

"A long time ago, many angels came down to earth. They fell in love with mortals and took mortal women as their wives. They lived on earth and had children. These children were half angel, half human. We are their descendants, the Guardians."

Trinity gasped.

"As part angel we are ordained to guard certain places on the earth from being used by demons as portals," Naomie continued.

"Are you telling me I am part angel?" Trinity asked, incredulously.

"Yes my child. You and Nicholas are part angel. It's where your gifts come from. Gifts you haven't even discovered yet, I am sure. But make no mistake, you are full human. You just have angel blood running through your veins."

Trinity felt like her head was going to explode.

She felt light headed.

Thud!

She hit the floor.

Chapter Thirty-Four

Everything was blurry.

Trinity opened her eyes to see the ceiling of the cottage above her. She was on the floor in Nicholas' arms.

"What happened?" she asked.

"You passed out," Nicholas whispered, gently.

"So, me, you, Guardians, half-angels, special powers, was that all real or a dream?" She asked.

Nicholas grinned.

"Real," she answered her own question.

Nicholas slowly helped her sit up. Once she sat up she brushed her hair out of her face.

"Nicholas?" she asked.

"Yes."

"We..."

"I know..."

"You think?"

"Yes."

"Wow."

"Exactly," he finished.

Sam looked at the twins confused.

"What were you two talking about?" he asked.

"They do that," Logan said.

"They know what the other one is thinking?" Sam asked.

"Pretty much."

Sam was amazed. One word and they could finish each other's sentence.

"You feeling okay now dear?" her grandmother asked.

"Yes, thank you," Trinity said. "So to recap, basically, I am a descendent of angels and humans and Nicholas and I have a great purpose here," she rambled.

"Trinity and Nicholas, this is a great honor," Naomie said. "Your life has purpose. There are great things you will accomplish in your life. But let's not get ahead of ourselves. We have a battle ahead of us here at Stonehenge and we need your help."

Trinity and Nicholas leaned forward listening.

"Darkness is a contagion," said their great-grandmother. "It spreads. But so does light. We are the danger to the darkness. It fears us. Where there is light, there can be no darkness."

Trinity thought she understood. Her great-grandmother stood up from her stool and kissed each of the twins on the forehead.

"God be with you," she whispered.

They left.

Trinity did not say anything on the train ride home. She sat in silence looking out the window. Today had been little surreal. Okay, a lot surreal. Logan sat quietly beside her, her brother and Sam in the seats across from them. Trinity did not look at them.

A thousand thoughts ran through her head. She was part angel, yet she was mortal. She had some supernatural powers, but she did not even know what they all were. Could a mortal angel and an immortal angel make a life together? If so, who did she love? If she was in love with two people at the same time, was she really in love at all?

Her mind raced. She could not find answers to any of her questions. This new information left her with more questions, not fewer.

Trinity walked to her room and closed the door. She had spoken to no one. She took out her diary and started writing down her thoughts, trying to make lyrics from them. This was her outlet. Her way to make sense of all the jumbled thoughts in her head.

After dark she heard a knock on her door.

"Come in," she said. Sam entered.

"You okay?" he asked.

"I guess."

"A lot to take in for one day," he said.

She nodded. He sat across from her on the window seat.

231

Silence.

"In a couple days we all need to move out to Stonehenge. Do you want to stay in the hotel provided by the competition or with your great-grandmother? She has offered to host us all.

"In her little cottage?" Trinity asked, amazed.

"She has another cottage behind it where we would all stay," Sam said.

"Who is we?" she asked.

"You, Nicholas, Me, Logan, Tristan, Alaina and Phoenix."

"Okay. Let's stay there. My parents will be coming out the day of the competition."

Plans were set.

"You feel like eating?" Sam asked.

"Sure."

"Why don't we go to that little Indian place we like?" Sam suggested.

"Where is Logan?" she asked.

"He is gone," Sam said.

"What?" she asked, hurt.

"It was an emergency," Sam said. "He will meet us at Stonehenge in a few days."

She did not like it but she understood. Was it always going to be like this?

The two of them walked to the cozy little eatery they liked so much. They took a table in the corner. It was a small place, with brick walls, candlelight and a rich but homey atmosphere.

Neither talked for a while.

232

"So go ahead, unload. What do you think about all this?" he asked.

"Overwhelming," she answered honestly.

He nodded, waiting for her to continue.

"I'm a Guardian. Descendant of angels and mortals. I knew that when Logan and the others came to our school last year, our lives were intertwined. I could feel it," Trinity rambled.

"It's kinda cool," Sam said, with a grin.

She smiled shyly. "Ya, it is."

The rest of the evening they talked about the upcoming battle. Trinity wanted to know how she and Nicholas were going to be involved. They were Guardians, but what exactly did that mean? Was she going to fight? She did not know how to fight.

"When the time comes, you will be prepared," Sam assured her.

"You better be right," she warned.

He grinned.

After dinner they walked home. They walked by a busy little pub. Patrons loitered in the street with full glasses. Groups of friends laughed and told loud stories. Trinity loved London at night.

"Well looky what we have here," she heard Roan say.

She turned and saw him leaning against one of the old buildings. He dropped his cigarette and put it out with his boot.

Sam instinctively stepped in front of her. Trinity smiled at Sam's protective nature, but stepped out from behind him.

"What are you doing here?" Trinity demanded.

233

"Just wanted to see the newest Guardian up close and personal," Roan leered.

Trinity and she flew at Roan, and shoved him hard in his chest. "You knew this whole time didn't you?" she said, accusingly.

Roan grinned. "Of course we knew."

"It's why you've been following me, watching me." She shoved his chest again.

"Feisty today," Roan crooned. "I like it."

"I am a descendant of immortals and you didn't want me to find out, did you?" she asked, sternly, right up in his face.

"It was my job to keep you from finding out. I failed," he said, seriously.

"Are you now going to leave me alone?" she asked.

"Ah Pet, never." He grinned.

"All right," Sam said, moving toward Roan. "That's enough."

Roan winked at Trinity.

"That's my cue, Pet."

He left.

Chapter Thirty-Five

Trinity knew she was dreaming. She was in a dark, underground tunnel illuminated by wall sconces of fire, not electricity. She looked down and saw that she was wearing black leather pants, a black and red corset with a shredded T-shirt underneath. She had two sheathed swords attached to each thigh. Weird. Very awesome, but weird.

She instantly recognized that this dream was different than the rest. She heard her name whispered.

"T-R-I-N-I-T-Y."

She drew the weapons from the sheaths at her side. They were nasty-looking swords. Each had two blades, and tips that could pierce through even the strongest armor. Trinity was startled that the weapons felt so natural in her hands.

She slinked along the tunnel and found a strange symbol carved into the wall. It looked like calligraphy with strange flourishes. But it was no letter she recognized. She noticed the stone that bore the symbol was loose and she pulled on it. As she did, she heard her name called again.

She spun around, swords ready.

A beautiful woman stood in front of her. She had flowing red hair and a tattoo on her arm of a Phoenix. She was dressed in a black vest and black leather leggings. The two stared at each other.

"Trinity," the red-haired woman said.

"Who are you?" Trinity asked.

Trinity bolted awake. She was in her room, lying in bed in a cold-sweat. Adrenaline coursed through her veins. This dream was important, but she was not sure why. She looked around. Everything was in order. Her parents were away for the weekend. So Sam, Nicholas and Trinity were there by themselves.

She lay back down and tried to steady her breathing. She looked out the window and saw London sleeping. She knew Sam was in the next room and would protect her from anything that threatened her life. She began to breathe easier.

It was another dream. She was in her room in bed. Someone sat beside her brushing wisps of raven hair from her face. She heard her name whispered sweetly. She sighed.

"It's time, Pet," someone said, softly.

Strong arms lifted her out of her bed. The movement was swift and gentle.

Trinity wondered if she really was dreaming. It felt so real. She could not wake up. She tried to force her eyes open, but they were too heavy. She moaned.

"Everything's going to be okay, Pet," the tender voice said.

She tried to wake herself up. It was a struggle, like wading in waist-high sand.

"Wake my sweet," said the voice. "Struggle. Fight me."

Suddenly she recognized that voice. She bolted awake, cold sweat running down her forehead Trinity was cradled in Roan's arms. He was expeditiously carrying her down the stairs. There were three other demons waiting at the base of the stairs. She was being kidnapped!

She could not find her voice. She was trapped inside.

She screamed within.

"SAM! Help!"

With a flash of light, Sam was in the family room. He was radiant, ready for battle. He was bare-chested with muscles defined and surging. He wielded his sword with ease.

"Put her down, Roan!" he demanded.

Roan did not move. The other demons drew glowing red swords and daggers. They stepped between Sam and Roan.

Trinity struggled against Roan's firm grip.

"Where are you taking me?" she asked.

"You don't think I was really going to let you make it to Stonehenge, do you?" Roan sneered.

Sam leaped at the first demon instantly slashing him into two pieces. The bisected demon vanished into smoke.

Two demons remained, and Roan, who still held onto Trinity.

Nicholas came running down the stairs and stopped when he saw the scene before him. He was helpless. There was not much he could do.

Sam fought the two demons. One wielded a glowing red sword while the other held two daggers.

Sam was mighty with his sword. But they were no match for Sam. She felt safe, even in the grips of Roan.

While Sam battled the two demons, Roan moved out the front door with Trinity over his shoulder.

She prayed. "Give him strength. Give him victory. Defeat the enemy."

"Hush up!" Roan sneered at her.

With a supernatural bound, Roan leaped from the ground to the roof of the building. He ran across the rooftops, putting distance between him and Sam. He knew the two demons would not defeat Sam, but they were buying him critical time.

Suddenly, Trinity saw a flash of light. Roan came to a sudden halt.

Samuel.

"Release the Guardian!" she heard him say.

Apparently Sam had dispatched the two demons faster than Roan anticipated.

"You know I can't do that," Roan said.

"Are you willing to die for this?" Sam asked, seriously.

Roan stood, silent.

"Roan, he's gonna kill you," Trinity said, still slung over his shoulder. "He just wasted three of your buddies back there."

Trinity lifted her head and blew a wisp of hair out of her face.

"At least put me down so the two of you can duke this out," she said. "You can't fight with me over your shoulder."

"You're insurance, Pet," said Roan. "He won't harm me with you covering half my body. What if he accidently cut your perfect little figure with his magical sword?"

Trinity had one move, but she was not sure it would work. She lifted her foot and swung it down hard until she made contact with his groin. Roan doubled over in pain and dropped Trinity. She slipped off the rooftop, falling head first to certain death.

Sam swooped down, his magnificent velvet white wings spread to full width. He caught her in mid-air and lifted her back to the rooftop. Roan had vanished.

"You had your chance to kill him, why didn't you take it?" she asked.

"If the choice is between saving you and killing Roan, I will save you every time," he said, his arm still wrapped around her. His wings floated gently behind him.

He took her breath away.

"Your wings are beautiful," she whispered, her fingers brushing gently over them. The night air was warm, but she shivered. Pulling her into his chest, he wrapped his wings around the both of them.

"Warm now?" he asked.

He wanted to lean down and kiss her, but he did not.

"We should get back," he said. "Hold on tight."

She wrapped her arms around him and pressed her head into his chest. They took off into the night air. It was as exhilarating as she remembered it when she flew with Logan.

Sam spired through the air, leaving her dizzy.

But within seconds it was over and they were back at their front door. Nicholas sat on the doorstep waiting, worried. He ran and embraced Trinity.

"I'd never forgive myself if anything happened to you," he said.

"I'm fine," she assured him.

They hurried into the house. When Trinity looked back at Sam his wings were gone and he looked like he had just woken up. No wings, no sword, no warrior, just Sammy.

"I can't go back to sleep," she said.

"I'll stay up and watch a movie with you," Sam offered as Nicholas hugged his sister and trotted off to bed.

"A movie sounds great," said Trinity. "As long as there are no angels or demons."

Trinity and Sam sat on the couch.

"You okay?" he asked, nudging against her shoulder with his. She nodded with a smile.

"So much for having a normal teenage life, right?" he joked.

"Normal is overrated," she smiled.

"You're right," he said. Messy makes life more interesting."

"Tonight was definitely messy," she said.

Sam yawned.

"Don't you fall asleep on me Superman," she teased.

"I'm tired," he said, with another playful nudge. "I just fought off four demons."

"I didn't think immortals got tired," she said.

"Fighting is hard work," he said, poking her cheek. "We aren't machines."

He yawned again and closed his eyes.

"If you fall asleep on me Sammy, I'm going to give you a permanent marker mustache," Trinity threatened grabbing a Sharpie from the table.

Sam grinned with his eyes closed.

"Maybe like Snidely Whiplash," she mused. "The black should look great with your blonde hair."

"No Hitler 'stache," Sam groaned, half asleep.

"Oh yes, you are getting a Hitler 'stache. That's even better," Trinity said with glee.

She snuggled into his side, a permanent marker in her hand, waiting.

"Make sure to check the mirror in the morning Sammy."

Sam mumbled something unintelligible and exhaled.

"That's right," she said in a soft baby voice. "Go to sleep. You are vewy, vewy, sweepy."

He passed out.

"Night night, Sammy," she whispered, with a mischievous grin.

241

She leaned over the top of him and carefully drew a mustache with the black marker. Trinity leaned back and looked at her work with pride.

"Sammy, I seriously mustache you a question," she said she giggled quietly. "But I'll shave it for later."

Then it occurred to her that payback might be fierce, so she hid the black marker so he could not do the same to her. Then she curled up on the other couch and went to sleep.

"Night night Sammy."

Chapter Thirty-Six

Sam yawned and saw Trinity curled up on the other coach. He vaguely remembered some playful threat last night about marker mustaches. He ran quietly to the mirror to see. Sure enough, he had a black marker mustache. He chuckled and decided to return the favor. He found a black marker, carefully sat on the couch next to Trinity and drew on her upper lip.

Her nose twitched a few times in her sleep as the pen tickled her upper lip. Then just as he finished, her eyes popped open. She saw him leaning over her, marker in hand.

"You didn't!" she exclaimed.

He grimaced.

"Oh, but I did."

She ran to the mirror. He followed, wanting to see her reaction when she saw his handy work.

She giggled at her reflection.

"You forgot something," she said, and grabbed the marker from his hand. Looking into the mirror, she drew a curlicue on each end of her marker mustache. She laughed at how mischievous it made her look.

He threw his arm around her shoulder, pulled out his cell phone and took a selfie of the two of them.

"I really wanted to go shopping for a new outfit for the concert," she said. "I guess I'm going like this."

"I'll go with you," he offered. "After all, two mustaches are better than one."

She grinned.

As she ran up the stairs she noticed a red rose on the coffee table. She paused on the steps, then turned around and went back down the stairs.

The note read, "To the new Guardian." She was still unsure who was sending them. She assumed it was Logan.

"Who else would send me flowers?" she thought to herself.

Trinity walked downstairs, ready to go shopping. Sam noticed the red rose in her hand.

"Another one?" he asked.

She shrugged.

Nicholas was still asleep so they left him a note. If he wanted to join them later he could call them.

Trinity and Sam began the hunt for a fabulous new outfit for Trinity's big night. She had not decided if she wanted to wear a dress, a tulle skirt or leather black pants. They had fun wandering through alternative shops, trying on outlandish hats and clothes.

Trinity found a black tulle skirt that was short in the front and long in the back. She purchased tights with horizontal stripes, alternating between solid black and sheer black. She also found the most amazing black and red corset she could wear over a shredded black shirt she already had.

When she tried it on, Sam's eyes eyebrows raised in admiration. She knew she had a winner.

People stared at them as they goofed around with their drawn-on mustaches. Trinity bought an oversized black top hat with a wide red sash around it. With her mustache and top hat she felt like a fashionable Londoner.

They ate lunch outside in Leicester Square. They split a pizza. Trinity laughed as a long piece of cheese stretched between her mouth and the piece of pie. Sam grabbed the cheese and popped it in his mouth. She grinned. She was happy the awkwardness was gone. They were pals again.

After lunch they walked back to the house. There was much to be done before they took the train to Stonehenge tomorrow.

As they walked back Trinity drew quiet.

"What's up, pal Trinity?" Sam asked, brushing his shoulder against hers.

"Just thinking that once again my premonitions came true," she said.

"The dreams you had this summer about Roan kidnapping you?" he asked.

She nodded.

"They don't happen exactly like they do in my dreams," she said.

"It is called foreshadowing," he explained. "It's quite the gift you know. You have the ability to see something that will happen and prepare for it." Sam told her.

"It's a little scary," she whispered. "I fear it."

Sam stopped walking and turned her towards him, his hands on her shoulders.

"Don't fear it," he said. "Embrace it. Appreciate it. Fear will turn your gift into something ugly. Understanding your gift will free you from any fear."

She just stared at him wondering if she would ever be able to embrace this "gift."

"It will take some time," he said, trying to alleviate her concern. "Don't worry, it doesn't have to happen overnight."

"You reading my thoughts?" she asked.

"Nope."

"Hmmm." she mused.

"Honest."

"I still think you immortals can read our thoughts," she said, suspiciously.

"We can't."

"Hmmm." She eyed him carefully.

"Scouts honor," he said, throwing up two fingers.

"You were never a scout."

"I know."

"Doesn't count," she teased.

"Okay…immortal honor?" he asked, taking a step closer.

"Hmmm."

"That doesn't do it for you?" he asked, playfully hurt.

She shrugged, playing it up.

"Sammy honor," he whispered, looking into her eyes.

She smiled and nodded. "That does it."

He grinned, resisting the temptation to cup her chin and kiss her cherry red lips.

Silence.

"Let's get back to the house," she said, quietly. It was starting to get a little awkward.

He poked her cheek.

Chapter Thirty-Seven

Great-grandmother Naomie greeted them at her door. She showed them to the little cottage behind her house. Nicholas, Trinity, Sam, Logan and the other three angels would use this as their base of operation through the concert and the battle to come.

From where she stood, Trinity could see stage crews setting up the lighting for the concert. She wondered when the demons would attack and if it would interrupt the show. She was nervous.

"Relax, you'll be great," Nicholas assured her.

Trinity grinned.

"I'm not nervous about the performance," she explained. "Just the army of demons mounting up behind the portal."

"Will everyone be able to see the demons entering the portal?" she asked Sam, looking up at the sky.

"Some," he explained.

"Will I be able to see them?" she asked. "Will the Guardians be able to see them?"

"Yes," he answered.

"So if I'm fighting a demon I might look like a crazy person fighting an invisible opponent?" she asked.

"Not quite," he answered. "You might actually move between realms as you fight, so people wouldn't necessarily see anything."

"Ok this just got weird," she said.

"Some things can't be explained logically," he said. "They just are what they are."

"I want to go for a walk," she said and walked down the sheep path towards Stonehenge.

Sam followed. They wound up sitting on a grassy bank at the foot of Stonehenge.

"It feels heavy," she mused.

"The atmosphere?" Sam asked.

"Ya."

"You are feeling the oppression," he explained. "The hordes of demons gathering at the portal," he explained.

She looked up to the sky.

"Will they come from above?" she asked. "Will the sky split open? Or will they come from below in the center of the Stonehenge rock formation? What's gonna happen here?"

"You'll have to wait and see," he said.

Trinity smacked him.

"Really, you aren't going to tell me their entrance plan?" she asked, playfully. "How am I supposed to help if I don't even know where they will be coming from?"

"When they come, you'll know what to do," he assured her.

"Oh gee thanks, that's encouraging," she said, sarcastically.

He poked her cheek. She gave him an annoyed look and poked his dimple.

They laughed together.

Lightening flashed.

The two stopped and looked toward the sky. A dark shadow slipped through a thin slash in the sky and flew down field. Sam and Trinity stood up immediately. He grabbed her hand and they ran down the field in the direction where they had seen the black creature fly.

"You have wings," she yelled as they ran. "Use them!"

"Too obvious," he yelled back as they rounded a barn and halted.

They saw a well-built, middle-aged man wielding a silver sword. He had just slashed the black creature into two halves. The creature disintegrated in a puff of smoke.

"Kiwi John," Sam acknowledged the Guardian.

"One slipped through already," Kiwi John said in a thick New Zealand accent.

"The first of many," Sam said.

Kiwi John slipped the sword into a tiny sheath on his belt. The massive blade disappeared into a pouch the size of a utility knife. Trinity stared amazed.

"Probably be a few more stragglers before the big night," Kiwi John said. "We've been keeping watch twenty-four hours a day, just in case something like this happened."

Kiwi John extended his hand out toward Trinity. "You must be Trinity."

She shook his hand.

"Nice to meet you Kiwi John," she said.

"We've been waiting for you and your brother," Kiwi John said. "Welcome to the party."

She was not sure how important she and Nicholas were. She guessed they would soon find out.

"John is a Guardian," Sam said.

"I figured as much," Trinity teased. "The sparkly sword was a give-away."

"Ah the toys," John said, with a lopsided grin. "One of the perks of the job."

"When do I get to accessorize?" Trinity asked Sam.

Sam grinned. "All in good time, Teacup."

"We will see you later at the meeting," Kiwi John said, waving as he turned to go.

Sam and Trinity walked back to the cottage.

"Wow," Trinity said, wide-eyed. "This just got real."

Sam looked at her reassuringly. "You can handle it. You were born for this."

251

"I'm glad you're here, Pal Sammy," she said, playfully pushing into his side.

"I'm glad you're here," he pushed back.

Later that night, Sam, Nicholas and Trinity entered a large barn where the Guardians were gathered. When Trinity and Nicholas entered, the barn became suddenly quiet. Naomie approached them and gave them a big squeeze. She led them the chairs at the front.

"These are my great-grandchildren, Nicholas and Trinity Heart," she introduced them to the room.

Sam did not need an introduction, everyone simply nodded and he nodded back.

"Welcome," one of the Guardians said. He seemed to be one of the lieutenants.

The twins nodded. This was overwhelming.

The Guardian lieutenant continued the discussion that had been interrupted by the twins' entrance. They were organizing a twenty-four hour watch schedule. Trinity, Sam and another Guardian named Clay were given a shift together. Nicholas was assigned a shift with two other Guardians. Since Trinity and Nicholas were new to the Guardians, they paired them with more experienced warriors.

On the night of the big concert, Trinity, Nicholas and Sam would not have any duties. At least until all hell broke loose. Literally. Trinity needed to be free to perform without any distractions, as silly as that sounded with everything going on.

The Guardians would be posted around the concert, ready to fight. They knew there would also be an army of angels waiting, ready to fight as well.

Before Trinity realized what was happening, each Guardian lit a candle and walked out of the barn. Trinity and Nicholas followed. Their grandmother handed them each a candle.

"What's going on?" she whispered to Sam, as they followed the others into a field.

Surrounding the field there were large mounds, six to ten feet high. Here were buried the mortals that been used as host by the demons the last time the portal opened.

"This is a ceremony to remember the humans that passed before you," Sam explained.

The Guardians circled in the dark, candles lit. Naomie began chanting. The other Guardians followed her lead. Trinity felt as though the stars directly above them were brighter than the rest of the sky. Truly a strange phenomenon.

"Bless those that came before us," Naomie chanted. "Bless our ancestors who fought to save the human race. Protect those who will be here. Guard them against the Dark Ones."

Trinity bowed her head. Many lives were taken at the last portal opening. The hundreds of burial mounds in the miles around Stonehenge were a constant reminder of those humans whose bodies were taken as hosts but did not survive. Trinity prayed this time would be different.

253

Once the ceremony was over, many of the Guardians introduced themselves to the twins. They hugged their great-grandmother and walked back to the cottage.

Nicholas' watch shift was at midnight and Sam and Trinity would take over at 3am. The three of them curled up around the stone fireplace in the cottage. Trinity snuggled under a quilt made by her great-grandmother. She traced her fingers over the different patches. She had learned that each square was from a different Guardian family. It was a quilt that would be passed down to her as the next female Guardian in the family.

"Does Nicholas get a toy?" Trinity asked Sam.

As if on cue, Naomie knocked on the door and let herself in.

"Hello my darlings," she greeted them.

She carried two wood boxes. She set the boxes down on the coffee table in front of them.

"I come bearing gifts."

Naomie opened one of the boxes and handed Nicholas what looked like a small utility sheath. Trinity recognized it at once and smiled. Kiwi John had one just like it.

Nicholas held it in his hand, not sure what it was.

"Carefully put your palm on the handle," Naomie told him. "And pull the sword from the sheath."

Nicholas looked confused. He did not see a sword. He was holding a four inch handle protruding from a three inch sheath. Trinity and Sam backed up. They both knew exactly what was going to come out of the sheath.

Nicholas did what he was told, and his eyes lighted up as he pulled a full-sized sword from the tiny scabbard. The sword glowed, illuminating the entire room. Nicholas wielded it with care and then put it back in the sheath, the entire length of the sword disappearing.

Trinity waited for her new gift. Her grandmother handed her two black sheaths.

"Two?" Trinity said, with glee.

Naomie nodded. She strapped a black belt around Trinity's waist, a black sheath hanging from each hip. The end of each sheath had a narrow leather belt that strapped the sheaths tightly to her thighs.

"You can wear it over your pants or under your skirts," her grandmother told her.

It was who Nicholas backed up when Trinity put her palms on both handles. She carefully drew the swords. Her weapons were dual blade swords about two-thirds the length of Nicholas' sword.

"Just like my dream!" she thought to herself, as she felt the weight in her hands.

They were magnificent! Trinity handled them around with ease. She was surprised at how natural they felt in her hands, like she had handled them all her life. She slipped them back in their sheaths simultaneously.

Naomie kissed each of her grandkids. "My darlings you are now armed. Wield your weapons with confidence." She left the twins with their new toys.

Trinity jumped up and down with glee. "These are so amazing!"

"Will they really kill demons?" she asked Sam.

"Yes, just like Kiwi John's," Sam said.

"How will we know how to fight?" she asked.

"You are a Guardian. You have a natural ability to fight," Sam assured her.

Trinity looked skeptical.

"You saying I'm magically going to know how to kill demons?" she asked, eyebrows arched.

"Pretty much," Sam said, grinning broadly.

Trinity rolled her eyes.

"You better be right, Pal Sammy."

Sam then spent the next few hours teaching them how to best use their new toys. As expected, the twins were naturals.

It was not long before Nicholas' watch partners knocked on the door. Nicholas followed them out the door, a silly grin on his face, but trying to act cool.

Trinity curled back up on the couch with her quilt.

"I'm going to get some sleep before our shift," she told Sam.

He sat on the other end of the couch and leaned his head back.

"Be careful not to accidently draw your swords in your sleep," Sam said.

Trinity grinned, half asleep. "Maybe you should sleep with one eye open, just in case."

Chapter Thirty-Eight

The night sky was filled with stars.

Trinity wore a red corseted dress with a full tulle skirt. She found herself in the center of the stones at Stonehenge, laid out on the altar stone. She tried to get up but she was strapped to the stone. Panic seized her.

Then the sky darkened. The clouds moved rapidly, as if they were on fast-forward. Trinity searched frantically, trying to find a way to break free from the straps that bound her. She felt for her weapons but they were not there.

There was a flash and a gap in the sky opened. Hordes of demons flew through the slash. Their leather skin gleamed in the night, their gruesome teeth gnashed, and their beady red eyes glowed.

Trinity cried out in fear. "Please help me!"

The demons flew straight down from the sky towards her, thousand in a tight formation. She felt her body open as if to accept the demons.

She screamed!

As they reached her, she closed her eyes and braced for impact.

Nothing happened.

When she opened her eyes, Sam was kneeling over the top of her with one hand and a knee braced against the altar stone. He held his other hand to the sky where a supernatural shield of light protected them from the rush of demons. As each Dark One struck the shield of light, it disintegrated in a flash. As more demons struck the shield, the light grew brighter. It was like looking directly into the sun.

Trinity turned her head to avert her eyes from the brightness. Sam's arm was inches away from her face, trembling under the force of thousands of demons. But he held strong.

Every one of the demon horde hit Sam's shield of light and disintegrated until they were all gone. With trembling hands, Sam cut the binds that held Trinity and lifted her with ease from the altar stone and set her on her feet.

They stood in the center of Stonehenge, his strong arms wrapped around her while the wind whipped her red dress around her knees.

Once again he had rescued her.

Trinity could hear her own pulse in her head, beating wildly like a drum. Sam's bare chest rose and fell as he breathed, recovering from the exertion.

She looked up into Sam's face. His eyes were hard as steel and his wings had appeared behind him, rising and falling rapidly in sync with his breathing. His body trembled.

Trinity watched awestruck. Sam was created for battle. This was his true self, at this moment.

Suddenly everything began to grow cloudy. Sam disappeared and the scene around her dissipated.

She cried out.

"No!"

She woke with a start.

Sam was by her side, patting her cheeks, trying to wake her up. Cold sweat soaked her face and back.

"It was just a dream," he assured her. "It was just a dream."

Her breath was shallow and quick. She realized she was panicking. She tried to take a deep breath.

"That's right," he told her. "Just take slow deep breaths."

Sam held her hand until she calmed and regained her senses.

"What time is it?" she asked.

"Time for our watch," he told her. "If you aren't ready someone else can fill in for you tonight."

"No," she said. "I want to do this."

259

She washed her face and put on a jacket. She tightened the straps securing her weapons over her leather pants. She was ready to take on the creatures of the night.

Sam gave her hand a little squeeze as they walked out the door to meet Clay.

"I kind of feel like I'm meeting a celebrity," Clay said shyly to Trinity as they approached.

"Who? Me?" she asked.

"You're the twins," Clay said, nervously. "I mean *THE* twins. Our ancestors prophesied you would come. You're the ones who will find the relic and restore the key to Stonehenge, closing the portal for eternity."

"Wow, talk about pressure," Trinity grinned. "Let's just get through tonight."

Clay was a few years older than Trinity. He had wavy brown hair and bright green eyes. He was cute, at least for a mortal.

The three of them sat on a stone wall across the road from Stonehenge, watching the night sky.

Trinity told Clay the story of how she met Logan and the other angels. She told him about Roan and the Dark Ones at her school. When she got to the part of her story where Roan had torn into her flesh and almost killed her, Clay stared at Trinity, mouth agape.

"Wow," said Clay, clearly star struck at Trinity's adventures. "I wish something exciting like that would happen around here. We haven't had any action around here, until now."

"Exciting?" said Trinity with a wry grin. "I wouldn't call having a demon tear holes in your body with his sharp fangs exciting."

Clay was oblivious to her point. "Can I see your scar?"

She lifted her shirt and pointed at the tattoo of a black feather that took the place of where the scare would have been.

"The angels healed me," she said.

Clay stared at Trinity, then looked at Sam.

Sam winked at Clay. "Welcome to the show, kid."

Trinity felt a heaviness while they were talking and scanned the night sky. Everything was quiet and peaceful. She ignored the feeling for a moment and turned back to listen to Clay tell a story.

She felt a shock of electricity and jumped.

Sam noticed. "You okay?" he asked.

"I felt a shock," she said, confused. "Also, the air is very heavy."

Sam raised his eyes, searching for any gaps or alterations in the night sky.

He saw nothing.

Trinity jumped again.

"Another shock?" Sam asked.

She nodded and stood up on the wall. Something was wrong. She felt it.

She felt pressure, like she was standing inside a balloon and someone was pressing against her from the outside. It felt like the balloon was about to burst.

Sam and Clay watched Trinity and stood up as well. It was happening.

Flash!

The sky split open and four black creatures slipped through. Sam leapt off the wall and ran to intercept them.

Trinity and Clay were close behind.

The creatures flew towards them. Sam sprang into the air and took flight, baring his wings and weapon. He slashed into the first demon, cutting him in half before it dissipated into smoke. Trinity and Clay drew their weapons and pitched into the remaining demons that circled the sky around them.

Trinity's sword connected with one of the demons legs and the appendage disintegrated. Her demon was now wounded and she took the upper-hand. She swirled around, wielding her weapons with confidence. Trinity raised both swords high and wide, and with a guttural scream she brought both blades down on opposite sides of the demons neck, slicing through his neck like a pair of scissors. Trinity stood for a moment, her eyes wide and her nostrils flaring, breathing heavily.

Sam had dispatched two demons and Clay had handled the fourth. The three of them stood poised, waiting, weapons drawn.

"That was all of them," Sam finally said. "At least for now."

They put their weapons away. Trinity smiled. That was exhilarating. Clay beamed from ear to ear. He was excited to finally experience some action. All his life he had heard about his ancestors and the battles they had won. Now he was a part of making history. Someday they would talk about him. Some day they would tell stories about him and this battle tonight.

"Let's post watch again," Sam told them.

They had another hour on their shift and there was a chance that more demons could slip through.

As they took their places on the stone wall, adrenaline was running high for Clay and Trinity. They could not stop talking about the fight.

"You think those electric pulses you felt had something to do with the portal opening?" Clay asked Trinity.

"I don't know. What do you think Sam?" she asked.

He shrugged.

"Anything is possible," Sam offered. "When the portal opens and they cross into the mortal realm it's possible you feel a disturbance in the atmosphere."

Trinity hoped she would feel it again before any more demons came through. It was like an alarm system, a trip wire that alerted her to the enemy's presence.

The sky started to lighten and they knew the sun was coming. Trinity watched as the sky turned hues of pink and purple. She looked over at Sam who grinned at her. Nothing needed to be said. They both enjoyed sharing the moment.

Their shift was up, so the next Guardians relieved them of their watch. Sam told them about the four demons that had slipped through. They would be on guard.

Trinity unbuckled her scabbard and placed her swords in the wood box. She was not sure she could sleep with all the excitement. She curled up with her grandmother's quilt on the couch in front of the fireplace.

"I don't know if I can sleep," she said, as she yawned and closed her eyes.

"Just try," Sam encouraged.

Two minutes later she was dreaming about cutting the heads off demons.

Chapter Thirty-Nine

Trinity woke mid-afternoon. Sam was curled up on the other end of the couch. She poked him with her foot.

"Hey sleepyhead," she teased. "Wakey wakey."

He yawned and stretched.

"That was a fun night," she said.

He chuckled.

"It's all fun till those things over-power you," Sam told her, seriously.

"I know. I've been there," she said quietly, feeling her side where Roan had torn her flesh.

Sam scooted and put his hand on her ankle.

"I'm sorry, I forgot," he said, comforting.

"There wasn't much that could have been done," she explained. "Logan was fighting the others when Roan attacked me."

"I needed to get there faster," Sam said, ashamed.

"What do you mean?" Trinity asked, wide-eyed.

Sam's head was down. He could not meet Trinity's eyes.

"Hey, whatever it is, it's okay," she said, trying to comfort him.

He slowly looked up at her exquisite face. He saw understanding in her blue eyes. Even after sleeping on the couch she was beautiful.

"Logan called for my assistance that night," Sam started to explain. "He wanted me to come watch over you."

"Oh," Trinity said, quietly.

"I was on my way, but it took me a while to get to you."

Silence.

"I arrived," he said quietly. "But I was too late."

Trinity threw her arms around Sam's neck and hugged him tight.

"It's okay. I know that if you had been able to be there you would have protected me."

"That's just it," he said. "I should have been there."

"But you didn't know to come until Logan called you, right?" she asked.

"Course not. When he called, I flew as fast as I could," he said.

"So you were there that night?" she whispered.

266

"I arrived after Roan had attacked you. I helped Tristan and Logan defeat the demons and then I was quickly dispatched to another location. I saw you that night, but I never met you. You were not conscious," he said.

She smiled at him.

"I'm glad I've met you now," she said, shyly.

"That night you were the most beautiful thing I had ever seen. It tore me apart that I wasn't able to save you from Roan's attack," he told her. "When Logan asked me to watch over you this summer, I jumped at the chance to redeem myself."

She smiled.

"It's why you are so ferocious when I need defending isn't it?" she asked.

"It's my job. I'm wired to protect," he told her. "I just didn't expect this…this…friendship," he said, gesturing to her cuddled up near him. "I wasn't actually supposed to meet you. I was supposed to…well…hover."

"Creepy," Trinity laughed. "That wouldn't have lasted long and you know it. I sensed you, I knew you were there."

"Yes and you insisted I show myself," he reminded her with a wry grin.

"You didn't have to," she said. "You could have remained invisible."

"But I kinda wanted to," he said, sheepishly. "I wanted to meet you, to get to know the beautiful girl that wasn't afraid to fight demons."

She blushed.

There were voices outside coming towards the cottage. Trinity recognized her brother's and Logan's voices. The door burst open. Nicholas and Logan walked in, and Tristan, Phoenix and Alaina right behind them. They were moving into the little cottage with them.

Trinity jumped up and gave them all a hug.

"You excited about your performance tomorrow night?" Alaina asked.

"Yes. But the portal opening is kind of a bigger deal," Trinity said.

Alaina rolled her eyes. She understood.

"So I heard you got a little action last night on your shift," Logan said, addressing Trinity with a grin.

"I killed my first demon!" she exclaimed.

They all laughed at her excitement.

"Seems to have quieted down since last night," Tristan said. "After those few came through unsuccessfully I'm sure they are reassessing their attack plans."

Logan pulled Trinity aside.

"Any more dreams?" he asked.

She nodded and explained about the one she had last night. Sam overheard and stepped into the conversation.

"It was pretty intense. She woke up in a cold sweat," he told Logan.

"The demons can't enter you, you're a Guardian. You can't become a host," Logan insisted.

"So then why was I on the altar?" she asked.

"Maybe symbolizing a sacrifice of some sort," Sam said, unsure what to make of her dream.

"Remember, the dreams never happen the same way as they do in real life," she said.

"And it could have been just that, a dream," Logan said. "Not everything you dream is a foreshadowing of events to come."

Sam told Logan about Roan's attempt to kidnap Trinity. Logan just stared at Trinity the entire time. He shook Sam's hand and thanked him for watching over her, but she could sense tension.

The ethereal foursome unpacked their weapons and everyone walked around outdoors. The stage was set up. Crews were finishing setting up the lighting. Trinity had a rehearsal this evening on the stage. She was ready.

The atmosphere was calm. Even though the air was heavy, Trinity knew the demon forces would wait until the concert tomorrow night before bursting through the sky. Tomorrow night there would be plenty of human hosts.

As the sun started to set, all seven of them sat on the stone wall and watched. It was the last peaceful evening they had before the turmoil tomorrow. Trinity feared Stonehenge would never be the same. She looked down the line of all her friends and brother sitting on the wall and knew she was blessed. At this very moment in time, Trinity Heart was happy.

Trinity's rehearsal went seamlessly. She knew she was going to rock it tomorrow night. She just hoped she did not have to whip out her immortal weapons in the middle of the second chorus.

The entire group was gathered around a bonfire. Trinity snuggled under an afghan while her brother made s'mores.

"You ready for tomorrow night?" Logan asked.

She looked at him, eyebrows raised.

"We talking about the concert or the war?" she asked.

He chuckled.

"I was referring to the concert, but I guess both are relevant," he said.

"I'm ready for both. Just hoping they don't happen at the exact same time," she said.

"Understandable," he said.

"Your parents going to be here tomorrow?" Alaina asked.

"Yes," she said, quietly.

She had mixed feelings about it. On one hand she wanted to tell them to stay home. On the other she wanted them to see her perform. But at what cost? She feared for their lives.

Logan sensed what she was thinking and reached out to hold her hand. Sam saw the gesture and watched from the other side of the fire.

"So, we gonna sing Kumbaya or tell ghost stories?" Nicholas joked.

"We could tell you some ghost stories that would scare the crap out of you," Tristan said.

"I'm sure you could," Nicholas said.

"So Kumbaya it is," Sam said.

Everyone laughed.

Chapter Forty

Trinity slept in. She did not wake up until afternoon. She walked to the kitchen and found coffee. She needed it. They had stayed up until almost dawn.

Her parents would be at Stonehenge in an hour. She wanted to warn them and tell them to go home, but she knew she could not do that.

She dressed in black shorts, slouchy thigh-high gray and black striped socks and a fitted T-shirt. She threw her unruly, curly hair in a ponytail. She found her brother outside with Sam.

"Where's Logan?" she asked. The question cut Sam even though he knew it shouldn't.

"They had preparations to make," Nicholas said.

"What about you Sam?" she asked.

"My job is to protect you, remember?" he said.

She grinned. "You're going to have your work cut out for you today."

He grinned.

"I got this," he said.

The three of them went to meet the twins' parents.

When Trinity saw her mom she rushed to give her a hug.

"You excited honey?" her mom asked.

"So excited. Tonight is going to be amazing!" Trinity said.

Concern could be seen her face. Her mother mistook it for nervousness.

"Oh honey, you are going to be wonderful. Don't be nervous," her mom comforted.

"I'm not nervous at all," Trinity said.

She contemplated how to warn her parents about what might happen tonight. Nicholas took care of it.

"So mom and dad, there have been some terrorist-type tonight," Nicholas said.

"At the concert tonight?" their dad asked concerned.

Trinity thought her brother was a genius.

"Yes. And they have assigned security to guard Trinity and me. So if something happens we will be taken care of and will meet you back in London," Nicholas explained.

"So if something happens, you two need to get out of here as quickly as possible," Trinity said, knowing her mom would come looking for her instead of running to save herself.

"I would prefer to meet up somewhere here and then escape to London together," her mom said.

"Yes, but with us behind the stage and the security guards involved, they have their set escape route. We need to know that the two of you will get out if something happens because we certainly will be," Nicholas said.

Their parents understood but did not like it. Trinity was relieved to know that they would be leaving quickly if things got bad.

Trinity told her parents before she went on stage she wanted her parents to come backstage and give her a hug before she sang. They both agreed.

When the twins and Sam walked back to the house, Trinity held her brothers hand.

"I just got..." she started.

"...nervous," he finished.

"Not singing."

"No. The other thing."

"What if?"

"Ya, I know."

"I feel like everything is going to change after tonight," Trinity said.

"I feel the same."

Trinity laid her head on her brother's shoulder.

"I hope mom and dad…"

"They'll be okay," he assured her.

"I'm not so sure."

Chapter Forty-One

Night had come. Trinity stood backstage nervous. She wore black leather leggings under a black tulle skirt. She had on a black and red corset over a shredded short sleeve knit shirt. This time she wore knee high lace up combat boots.

Sam had her weapons. He was not leaving her side. The moment any demons tried to come through the portal she would ditch her guitar and strap on her swords.

Nicholas held her hand. The first band went on stage. The crowd cheered. The music soared as the concert began. Sam stood to her side. Logan, the other angels and the Guardians were scattered around Stonehenge, on guard. Logan had come by to wish her luck and told her that there were a massive amount of Warrior angels at the concert ready for tonight's invasion through the portal.

Trinity looked skyward. It was midnight blue and the stars were out. Nothing looked menacing. She knew in a short time the sky would rip open, demons would pour through and all these people attending the concert were susceptible to becoming hosts for ghouls.

The first band finished. The crowd cheered. They were good, but Trinity knew she was better. Sam squeezed her hand. It was almost time for her to go on stage.

"Trinity!" her mom yelled from a distance.

The twins ran to their parents and gave them big hugs. Trinity did not want to let her mom go. She wanted to tell them to get on the train and go back to London right now.

"I love you," she whispered in her mom's ear. Her mom squeezed her back. Trinity leaped into her dad's arms and held him tight.

"I love you dad," she said.

He held her tight.

Sadness filled Trinity. She felt as though this was the last time she would see them. She feared the worst.

The stage director came and got her. It was time to go. She gave her brother a big hug.

"You're gonna be great!" he said.

She turned to Sam who grabbed her and gave her a big hug.

"Knock 'em dead, Pal Trinity," he whispered.

He poked her cheek.

She smiled.

She watched as her parents hurried to their seats so they could watch her. Trinity grabbed her guitar and walked out on stage. The crowd erupted. She could see her brother and Sam watching from the sidelines.

The lights dimmed. Dry-ice drifted across the stage. She began her set with a haunting melody. It began soft with just her and the piano. At the second chorus the song erupted into a rock ballad. She had an electric guitar solo. She gave her drummer a smirk. They were good and she knew it.

The second song was upbeat and gothic style rock. The lights strobe, she grabbed the microphone and sung her heart out. The crowd went insane.

For the moment she forgot about the demons waiting to burst through. Right now it was just her and the music.

It was obvious the crowd liked her more than the previous group. She finished her set with her favorite song that she had written. The stage lighting made everything more dramatic. She loved performing. Trinity and her band finished with a bang. The crowd went wild. They would not let her leave the stage. She kept taking a bow. Finally she was escorted off the stage but the crowd kept chanting her name.

When the announcer tried to introduce the next band, the crowd would not stop chanting her name. She felt special. They loved her. Her brother gave her a big hug.

"This is awesome!" he yelled over the crowd. Sam was there by her side and gave her a hug.

The crowd continued to chant T...R...I...N...I...T...Y.

Suddenly Trinity froze.

"Oh no!" she said, terror on her face.

"What's the matter?" Sam asked.

"It's gonna happen now!" she yelled.

"How do you know?" Nicholas said, looking around.

"They are chanting my name, just like Roan has done for the past year. I just know...it's now!"

Dry lightning flashed.

Trinity knew Logan could hear her prayers and she used it like a walkie-talkie.

"They're coming now. Give us strength and victory."

The sky ripped open. Trinity had never seen anything like it. A hoard of black, leathery beings flooded through the opening. The crowd screamed not sure what was going on. The angels transformed into angelic beings. Each of the Guardians drew their weapons and prepared for a fight.

Sam drew his sword and cut off Trinity's tulle skirt with the blade. Slightly dramatic and cliché, but effective. It would just get in her way. She buckled her weapons over her leather pants. The three ran to their assigned post.

The scene was mayhem: teenagers screaming, the sky flashing red, demons scattering about trying to take human hosts. The angels and Guardians began to fight off the demons, trying to save every human they could.

Trinity fought side by side with her brother, slashing demons as they tried to rip her to pieces. She came across Logan who had just saved a young girl from a demon trying to take her body as a host. The girl was relieved and crying. Trinity screamed at her to run. The girl grabbed her friends and obeyed.

A demon launched at Trinity, tearing into her back with his talons. She tried to roll him off but his sharp nails were embedded into her skin. She felt a thrust and she saw the demon disintegrate on her back. She turned. Sam had saved her.

"Hi," he said as he turned to fight off another demon.

She was amazed at his ability to make her smile in the midst of the turmoil. She slashed two demons that descended on two teens.

The battle waged. Trinity did not know where her parents were, but she hoped they had escaped.

Several teens were taken by demons. Trinity saw Guardians casting out the demons. The demons were removed and then slaughtered, the youngsters saved.

Her exhaustion was over-powered by adrenaline. Trinity kept fighting. She was fighting two demons when a third flew to high above her. The third demon swooped down like a bird of prey. She buried her swords into the two demons on either side of her. Sam jumped over her body, his sword extended, impaling the demon diving down on her and sending it to oblivion.

"Hi," she said.

Several humans had been taken over by demons and the Guardians were unable to remove them. The mortals died. Trinity

280

stared as she watched them crumple to the ground, their lives snuffed out by the demon. The sight shocked her. Sam saw her frozen, staring at the dead teenagers. He ran to her and threw his arm around her.

"Keep fighting," he said.

It seemed like the battle took hours, but it last only fifteen minutes. The numbers of demons dwindled. The angels were strong and victorious. A few angels were lost in battle. When they were killed they evaporated into plumes of bright light. There were mortals that were slain. They had not survived the demons trying to take their bodies as hosts. The Guardians would survey the damage when the fight was over. These mortals deserved a proper burial.

There were but a few demons remaining. Sam and Trinity waded into them ferociously, swords twirling like a blur. The other angels touched their swords together to create a silvery beam of light that extended upward to the heavens. It was the same light Trinity had seen in the woods back at school last year. The beam sealed the torn sky, keeping any more demons from entering.

Trinity was sweating and tired. She continued to fight valiantly and thrust her swords into two demons as Sam shielded her one last time and killed a third demon that tried to blindside Trinity. Then just as quickly as it started, all the demons were dead.

Trinity stood heaving. Sam looked down at her, inches from her face. He had proven his worthiness as her Protector.

She nodded at him in thanks.

281

"Thanks Pal Sammy," she said.

"It's Samuel."

"Nope."

"Sam?" he asked.

 "Sammy."

He grinned.

Chapter Forty-Two

The Guardians had lost several of their own. They moved the bodies to the center of Stonehenge to honor them. The Guardians and several of the angels that remained behind gathered the humans that had not made it.

The sight saddened Trinity. So many humans slaughtered at the hands of the demons because they could not successfully inhabit them.

Then Trinity froze.

"No!" she screamed.

She ran to two bodies that lay mangled and dead. She fell to the ground and pulled the shoulder of one of the bodies and turned it over. It was her mom.

"Ahhhhhh!" she screamed at the top of her lungs in agony.

Nicholas, Sam and Logan came running. When Nicholas recognized his parents, he threw himself at their bodies. Sam and Logan stood and wept, heartbroken for their friends.

The twins sobbed as they gripped the lifeless bodies of their mom and dad. The Guardians surrounded them, everyone kneeling and extending their hands to the twins in love and support.

"They deserve a Guardian burial," their great-grandmother said, softly.

Two Guardians pulled crimson blankets over the twins' parents. They carried them to Stonehenge where the bodies of the slain Guardians lay.

Trinity and Nicholas stayed with their parents bodies all night. They sat with their backs against one of the large stones and their knees pulled up to their chins. Nicholas had his arms wrapped around his sister as he comforted her.

Dawn was breaking. The Guardians and the angels gathered around those who had been slain in battle. Their bodies lay in the grass in the center of Stonehenge. Dozens of angels and Guardians circled Stonehenge. They clasped hands and made a ring.

Trinity's great-grandmother began to chant. Her pure voice cut through the morning air. Nicholas realized how much her voice sounded like Trinity's. Naomi performed the ceremony to honor the fallen Guardians. There would be a formal funeral later, but this was tradition.

Logan held her hand on one side, Nicholas on the other. Even through her loss, Trinity could see that this moment was beautiful and special. But she cried. She cried a river of tears for her loss. Although the world was saved, Trinity felt like her world was lost.

Afterwards, Trinity and Nicholas were escorted to the little cottage. Logan, Sam and the other angels accompanied them. Trinity and her brother lay down. They held each other and wept for her parent until they fell asleep.

When Trinity awoke, she dragged herself into the front room and curled up on the couch with a blanket. Sam brought her a cup of tea. It was past supper time.

"Thank you," she whispered.

He wanted to say something. To hold her and comfort her. But he did not. Logan was there.

Logan sat on the couch with Trinity and wrapped his arms around her. He stroked her hair and whispered comforting words to her.

"They're gone," she whispered, disbelieving.

"Yes."

"I was sure they had gotten away."

"I know."

"We've lost everything."

"You have me," her brother said from the doorway.

Trinity looked at him, relieved.

"You have me," Sam said, standing by the fireplace.

"You have all of us," Logan said.

"Yes I do," she said, with a weak smile.

Her grandmother came into the room. She brought a tray of food and placed it on the coffee table.

"Eat up," she said. "Ceremony is in an hour and you'll need to shower and get ready."

"Ceremony?" Trinity asked, beginning to eat.

"There is a Guardian ceremony this evening. You and Nicholas are the honored guest," Naomi explained.

"I'll leave out your garments," she said as she kissed her grandchildren on the head and left the room.

The twins ate and then readied themselves. Trinity was dressed in a taffeta dress and corset. They each were to wear a hooded, floor-length cloak. Nicholas' cloak was navy blue and Trinity's was crimson red.

Logan, Sam, Tristan, Alaina and Phoenix were seen as the angels that they really were. The boys were shirtless, dark leather pants, their bodies glowing. Alaina wore a green corset and leather pants.

They escorted the twins, carrying torches. They walked to the Stonehenge circle. The other Guardians were already there, each in a black cloak similar to the twins. Fire-lit torches illuminated the stones.

The sky was dark, but the stars were bright. The moon was full. The twins' great-grandmother started the ceremony. There was chanting and singing. They watched, wondering what exactly was going to happen. All the Guardians that had been slain were moved and their burials begun.

As the warmth of the singing and chanting enveloped her, Trinity became emotional. Tears streamed down her face. Though she had lost her parents and her world had changed forever, Trinity knew this was where she was supposed to be. This was her calling. In her veins ran the blood of mortals and of angels. She was a Guardian.

Trinity looked over her shoulder. Her five angel friends stood outside the Guardian circle. Their feathery and velvet wings waved in the wind. They were here to observe the ceremony. Trinity felt the presence of more than just those five. Somewhere in the sky, she knew there were hundreds of angels watching the two newest Guardians take their vows.

Her grandmother anointed both the twins and declared them Guardians. One by one, each Guardians came to Nicholas and Trinity, removed their hood and repeated the oath.

"Angels and mortals. Brothers and sisters. Sworn to be Guardians."

When every Guardian had sworn the oath to Nicholas and Trinity, it was their turn. Nicholas removed his hood and said the oath out loud.

Trinity removed her hood. Her cheeks were stained with tears. She whispered.

"Angels and mortals. Brothers and sisters. Sworn to be Guardians."

Chapter Forty-Three

The following morning Trinity got up and dressed in the usual plaid, pleated short skirt, thigh-high socks, shredded T-shirt and combat boots. Her hair was wavy and unruly. Her lips red and plump. Today, she was Guardian.

Trinity sat outside on the stone wall outside her grandmother's cottage. A lot had happened in just a few short days. Nicholas walked up and sat next to her.

"You okay?"

"I think so. You?"

"I think so."

"We're Guardians."

"I know."

Silence.

"You ready for this?" he asked.

"Ya," she said, with a smile.

"What next?" he asked.

"You two are being asked to fulfill the prophesy," their grandmother interrupted from behind them. She walked to them and placed a hand on each of their knees.

"Stonehenge portal needs to be locked. Right now, it's just closed, but this could happen again," their grandmother explained. "The prophesy foretold that one day twins would be born into a Guardian family and these twins would find the relic and restore the lost key to Stonehenge."

"The key will lock the portal forever?" Trinity asked.

"Yes. No demon will ever be able to use it as a portal again," their grandmother said.

"Where is the key?" Nicholas asked.

"It's been rumored that it is in Eastern Europe," Naomi told them. "It is up to you to find the key and return it to Stonehenge."

"Where does the key go to lock the portal?" Trinity asked.

"In the lock of course," their grandmother said, with a sly grin.

Trinity gave her grandmother a perplexed look.

"Do the two of you accept the mission?" their grandmother asked.

Nicholas looked at Trinity. Trinity looked at Nicholas.

"Yes!" they said in unison.

"Good," Naomi said and left the twins to ponder their future.

"Looks like you two have your work cut out for you," Logan said from behind them.

Nicholas looked back at him.

"Guess so," he said as he hopped off the stone wall and walked inside, leaving Logan alone with Trinity.

Logan leaned against the wall. Trinity hopped off and stood in front of him. She knew what she needed to do.

"We need to talk," she said.

He nodded.

"Logan," she began, unsure of herself.

"I think I know what you are going to say," he interrupted her, gently.

"What am I going to say?" she asked, her head tilted to one side.

"It's not meant to be," he answered, with a sad smile.

She grimaced.

"It has nothing to do with mortality or immortality. What we have is special and unique and I will always remember that my first love was a snow angel, my snow angel," she whispered.

"I know," he said, cupping her chin in his hand.

"I have feelings," she started.

"I know," Logan said, quietly. "He is a good angel. He will always be there for you."

"You know?" she asked.

"I can see it."

"I don't want to hurt you," she said.

"I am hurt," he replied. "But you did not hurt me."

"It's cheesy, but...you will always have a place in heart," she said.

"Ya I know. I understand," he said, as he touched the side of her face. "Trinity I want you to know, that I have enjoyed every moment we have spent together. I will always be here for you. If you ever have feelings again, I am here. You are the only mortal I have ever loved."

"Friends?" she asked, hopeful.

"Friends," he said, assuredly.

They hugged.

While still in his embrace she asked, "Were you the one sending me roses?"

He pulled back with a wry grin on his face.

"No. When did you get roses?" he asked.

"Every now and then I found one by my bed."

He looked confused. "Wasn't me."

She was perplexed.

"Sounds like you have a secret admirer," Logan said.

"Well I hope it's the angelic kind and not the ghoulish," she mused.

Logan laughed softly.

It was time for Logan to leave. He gave her one last look and walked away from her down the sheep path. She knew he would disappear once he was out of sight.

Trinity stood alone. She felt better. It was sad to let Logan go, but she knew she needed to. "Hey Pal Trinity!" Sam yelled out, breaking her thoughts.

"Hey Pal Sammy," she said, smiling.

He came over and hopped up on the stone wall. She joined him. He leaned his shoulder against hers.

"Hi," he said.

She grinned. He poked her cheek. She poked his dimple.

"Where's Logan?" Sam asked.

"It was time for him to go," she said, quietly.

"When will you see him again?" Sam asked.

"I don't know. We kinda...broke-up," she said, shyly. "We are still friends."

Sam tried not to show his excitement.

"Did you end it, or did he?" Sam asked.

"I did," she said.

Sam looked at her. She looked at him.

"You okay?" he asked.

"Ya."

"I heard you and your brother are going to go find the key."

"Ya."

Suddenly Trinity was sad. Was Sam going to have to leave as well? She was so used to having him around, she did not even think about the fact that he might have a different mission.

Sam leaned into her.

"I'm not going anywhere," he said with a grin.

"Hey!" she said, wondering if he could read her thoughts.

"I knew what you were thinking," he said.

"You coming with us?" she asked him, disbelieving.

"Sounds like you need a Protector angel."

"I do!"

"Then sign me up, I'm the guy for the job."

Trinity threw herself at him and hugged him. She released him. They sat silently on the stone wall.

"You okay…about your parents I mean?" Sam asked.

"I will be."

"So now that you're a Guardian, what do you think about all this angel and demon stuff?" he asked.

Trinity's eyes hardened and her jaw tensed. She lifted her chin confidently and whispered in a low voice.

"It just got personal."

About the Author

Julie Bragonier Minnick, is an author of young adult novels. She loves to explore the spiritual, the strange and the paranormal.

Julie plays and coaches roller derby on the West Coast, which means she hits girls on skates...just for fun.

She loves to travel and has a pair of "adventure pants" which usually gets her into sticky situations abroad, yet those precarious moments make delicious stories. Readers will experience the places she has been and the adventures she has seen when they read her novels.

In her spare time, Julie watches way too much reality TV. That means she sits on the couch mocking the girls who cry when they get kicked off The Bachelor...when they've only known the guy for two hours. (Yes she admitted to watching The Bachelor.)

Julie is also a fan of video games. Okay, she's actually an obsessive gamer chick.

Julie loves hearing from young readers, so send her an email at Julie@JulieMinnick.com.

Go to JulieMinnick.com to like her Facebook page.